# TEMPTING FATE

By

David F. Paulsen

Copyright © 2021 by David Paulsen
All rights reserved.
ISBN: 979-8524688576

# DEDICATION

To the good people of Chicago. Sorry I blew you up.

# CONTENTS

|  | Acknowledgments | i |
|---|---|---|
| 1 | Going Through The Motions | 1 |
| 2 | Beach Life | 6 |
| 3 | The Shoemaker Girls | 11 |
| 4 | Special Agent Toomey | 17 |
| 5 | A Pissing Contest | 21 |
| 6 | The Big One | 26 |
| 7 | My Kind of Town | 31 |
| 8 | Working For The Man | 34 |
| 9 | Taking Care of Business | 41 |
| 10 | Special Agent Chewy | 44 |
| 11 | Hurts So Good | 48 |
| 12 | Dead Drop | 52 |
| 13 | April In Chicago | 56 |
| 14 | The Siren's Song | 59 |
| 15 | April's Story | 62 |
| 16 | Chewy's Advice | 65 |
| 17 | First Date | 68 |
| 18 | April's Games | 72 |
| 19 | Meet Daryl | 74 |
| 20 | The Confrontation | 78 |
| 21 | The History Lesson | 82 |
| 22 | Closing In | 89 |
| 23 | Jihad is Hard | 92 |
| 24 | Because You're Worth It | 95 |
| 25 | The Promise | 98 |
| 26 | Future Shock | 101 |
| 27 | April's Fool | 105 |
| 28 | The Devil is in The Details | 108 |
| 29 | Let's Roll | 110 |
| 30 | Crunch Time | 114 |
| 31 | Doomsday | 116 |
| 32 | Aftermath | 119 |
| 33 | The Living Dead | 121 |
| 34 | A Few Modifications | 123 |
|  | Excerpt From Trusting Fate | 125 |
|  | About The Author | 132 |

# ACKNOWLEDGMENTS

I'd like to thank my lovely wife, Claudia, for providing me the encouragement as well as the time and space to write. She embodies the spirit that inspires my Jennifer character. No enhancements necessary.

Thanks also to the real professionals in the FBI and Homeland Security Department that do the hard work of keeping us safe from terrorism every day. Sorry about the Joe Friday references along with all the crazy acronyms.

As always, thanks to all the unnamed people in my life who make brief appearances throughout. Hopefully, you will recognize yourselves.

Save me
Save me from the nothing I've become.
- Bring Me to Life by Evanescence

# 1
# GOING THROUGH THE MOTIONS

Ever since Jennifer left things have been different. Chewy and I moved to California. No more hurricanes, just the occasional earthquake, drought, wildfire, and mudslide. We live near the ocean, north of the plastic craziness of LA and south of the socially conscious pretentiousness of Santa Barbara. Chewy likes the year-round cool ocean breezes and our morning walks on the miles of uncrowded beaches. Neither of us miss the incessant humidly, hordes of insects, and oppressive heat of South Florida. Not to mention the occasional catastrophic hurricane. We do however miss Jennifer. A lot.

My name is Jake Hedley. I'm just an ordinary guy who can sometimes do some not so ordinary things. The ordinary part of me does normal people things. I have a job, a few friends, and a dog named Chewy.

The not so normal part of me is known only to a few people - my best friend, my ex-girlfriend, and my dog. I can see the future. Yours, mine, or anyone's. You might think that with such an ability – a Gift you might call it – my life would be smooth sailing. And it might be except for a few issues. My gift comes with some rather significant limitations. First, I don't always see the future. I have to want to see it, with intention. It takes a certain amount of mental focus plus a rather annoying amount of eye twitching for me to see what's going to happen next. And frankly, most of the time, I'm just not that interested.

Which brings me to the second issue. I bet when you think of psychics and gypsies that tell your fortune, you expect them to tell you cool stuff about what's going to happen in your life over the next year or two. You know they're mostly full of shit, but you probably walk away thinking how insightful they seemed. And part of you is hopeful that maybe you really will meet that special person, or write that novel, or get that promotion this year. Unfortunately, my Gift is nothing like that. If I did your reading, you'd probably demand your money back. That's because when I look at your future or even my own, I can only see what's going to happen in the next twelve minutes. Unless you happen to be having a major life event in the next few moments, my reading of your future is likely to be less than satisfying. Now if you take me to the horse track or the craps table, things will get a bit more exciting. That's why I travel to Vegas with some regularity. A guy has to make a living somehow, I guess.

There are a few other aspects of my Gift that do get a bit more interesting. In addition to being able to take a twelve-minute peek at anyone's personal future, I can also see major world events that are going to happen up to twelve *days* into the future. The major world events that I see are focused on things that interest me or that will happen in my part of the world. It's not like I get to select which future events I see – they just appear to me as headlines in my mind. I call these headlines of major future events "Mega Events" since they impact far more than just a single person.

There is one other aspect of my Gift that is more than a little bit spooky. Under the right circumstances, I can *change* someone's future to something I like better. I can sometimes even change those Mega Events – just not as reliably. Messing with major world events is dangerous because the outcome is not strictly predictable. It's a bit like reshuffling the deck and hoping for a better card. I don't often do that unless, as my ex-girlfriend Jennifer says, the future outcome is so terrible that changing it to anything else would be better. She calls it a "morally unambiguous" decision. I've only done that a few times and never since leaving Miami.

Back in my Miami days, I used to work as a hurricane model forecaster at the National Hurricane Center (NHC). I used my ability to see the future to help predict tropical hurricanes. I'd regularly look at those Mega Event headlines up to twelve days into the future. Whenever I'd see a headline for a major hurricane, something like: **HURRICANE BOB STRIKES PALM BEACH**, I'd use those future details to update our hurricane model and improve its forecast accuracy. Combining my twelve-day peek into the future with our super complex computer model, made our NHC hurricane forecasts deadly accurate. We saved a lot of lives that way.

The only person who knows about my abilities besides Jennifer and Chewy is my friend Phil. Phil is also one of my former colleagues at NHC and oversees their premier hurricane forecasting model. Together we perfected a rather unorthodox technique of hurricane forecasting. We developed a secret "backdoor" to the hurricane model where Phil would enter the details from my peek into the future. On rare occasions, and only for morally unambiguous killer storms, I'd also use my ability to change the future to something less bad.

But now I'm out of the hurricane biz. I still help Phil during hurricane season so he can better forecast a particular storm. I never try to change them though. I don't want that kind of responsibility anymore. These days I'm a delivery driver for Amazon. It's the perfect no drama, low stress job.

No need to fuck that up by trying to change the course of the most powerful natural force on Earth, right?

I do use my "Gift" fairly regularly for other things. Mostly to meet women. There's a ton of local drinking establishments around here just swarming with single women. A typical night out for me goes something like this. I notice an attractive, hopefully single woman having a drink at the bar. Let's call her Hot Bar Girl. Rather than trying the same old tired pick-up lines (which unless you happen to be Brad Pitt or Ashton Kushner have a high failure rate), I use another approach. I take a quick peek at my own future, 12 minutes ahead. If the headline reads **Jake Picks Up Hot Bar Girl**, I just proceed as a guy normally would. If, however, the headline says **Hot Bar Girl Ignores Jake** or worse **Hot Bar Girl Throws Drink at Jake**, there's a decision to be made.

First, I look beneath those future headlines in my mind for details and any possible alternative outcomes. Maybe I notice that she's waiting for her boyfriend or perhaps has just recently killed her boyfriend. In that case, I'll either look around to meet someone else or leave the bar with a certain urgency depending on the situation. Alternatively, if I see that Hot Bar Girl is just being shy or playing hard to get or waiting for someone better, I may try something different.

I could just try changing up my actions and approach her a bit differently, but that almost never works. Here's the thing. Once I see an event in the future, it typically has a very high (say 95%) chance of occurring, no matter what. Fate does not like to be changed.

Instead, depending on my level of interest and the attractiveness of the woman in question, I may attempt to alter the future a bit. I do this by taking a closer look at those alternative outcomes that I see just beneath the original headline. There are gazillions of them – pretty much everything that could possibly happen for that event. Some wonderful, some tragic, and everything in between. I quickly sort through those alternative outcomes until I find one I like better. Let's say something like: **Hot Bar Girl Flirts with Jake**. Sometimes, if I'm lucky, there will be a little flashing button that appears on that outcome. That button tells me I can change the original outcome to this new one if I want. I press it in my mind and presto, whatever needs to happen to make that event happen, just happens. The next thing I know, I'm sitting next to Hot Bar Girl and she's flirting with me like crazy. Pretty cool right? It's a gift.

Unfortunately, many future events cannot be changed at the last moment like this, so often that little flashy button is grayed out. I think it's a bit like hypnotism. As any good hypnotist knows, you can only alter someone's behavior in the future if they're susceptible – in other words if they would have done that anyway under exactly the right circumstances. I just create exactly the right circumstances.

One unfortunate side effect of my peek into the future is this annoying eye twitch. Whenever I look at the future, my right eye starts twitching like crazy. Time slows down for me while I do this. What seems to me like hours of sorting through various future event headlines and alternative outcomes, actually takes only a second or two. All I have to do is keep my head down for a few moments to remain inconspicuous. Sometimes I forget though and people start looking at me like I'm having a stroke.

Now I know what you're thinking and it's not because I used any special abilities. Jennifer thought that too at first when I told her about my little "gift". You think that just because I tweak the future to *meet* a girl, maybe I'd also go farther and make her *sleep* with me too. I probably could do that if I wanted to - unless that wasn't a behavior in which she would normally engage. But I don't and I wouldn't. I do have a moral compass after all – even if I can't always remember where I put it. But meeting women at a bar is just a contrived social ritual and it serves no useful purpose. It's just a mating dance. I don't mind taking a few shortcuts around that. After getting past that initial step, I leave the rest up to fate. All I do is tempt fate a little.

These days the bar scene and the bedroom are about the extent of my female relationships. Jennifer's departure is still too fresh. Maybe it always will be. Still, I'm not complaining. At least I still have my dog.

My dog's name is Chewy. He's a talking Golden Doodle. He's one of a kind as far as I know. Chewy doesn't talk out loud, I hear him in my mind. I'm not sure how this works (or any of it really), but over the years I've come to accept many things I don't understand. Loosing Jennifer being the one exception. I haven't accepted that one yet.

According to Jennifer, Chewy is a real dog under the influence of an 11th dimensional entity – whatever that might be. And she would know, being one of those entities herself. Apparently, he's been assigned to me. In addition to all his normal doggie duties, Chewy has the extra assignment of being my guide. Or as he puts it, helping me stay out of trouble. The universe doesn't like leaving people like me free to roam around unsupervised. When Jennifer left, she told me to listen to Chewy and that someday he might guide me back to her. We're both still waiting.

Chewy: I miss Jennifer almost as much as I miss my balls.

Here I should mention that I had Chewy fixed a couple of years ago. He was humping all my household appliances, not to mention my girlfriend. Something had to be done. He's still not happy about it.

Me: Me too buddy. Me too.

Chewy: At least you still have your balls.

Me: True. At least there's that.

Chewy: Have you heard from her lately?

Chewy knows that Jennifer sometimes leaves me short notes when I check the future. They appear as single headlines mixed in with those foretelling future events. Things like: **Jennifer Says Hello!** It's not much but at least it keeps me connected to her in some small way.

Me: Not for a few days, no. I guess I'll check again tomorrow.

Chewy: Let's go for a walk on the beach. Maybe you'll meet some new bikini babe.

Me: It won't be Jennifer. It's never Jennifer. But we can go if you want.

Chewy says he'll recognize Jennifer by her smell if we ever run into her. She won't look like her or even have her same name, but Chewy will recognize her smell. She smells really good he says.

Chewy: Let's saddle up! You never know what kind of crazy bitches we might meet.

Me: Are we talking real bitches, you know the furry kind on four legs?

Chewy: Potentially, but that could also describe any number of your recent gal pals. Either way, I'm good.

We head off to the beach. It's only a short walk from my place. It's not allowed, but I let Chewy run free without his leash. It seems the least I can do considering the whole ball-ectomy thing. Chewy is a real chick magnet and in no time flat he's gathered a flock of eligible bikini babes for my enjoyment. He's running around making them laugh, but I can tell by his sad eyes that none of them are the girl we are really looking for. Still the sight of my dog running happy circles around a bunch of lovely ladies makes me smile.

David F. Paulsen

I been all around this great big world,
And I seen all kinds of girls,
Yeah, but I couldn't wait to get back in the States,
Back to the cutest girls in the world,
I wish they all could be California girls.
 - California Girls by Mike Love / Brian Wilson

# 2
# BEACH LIFE

I do have a friend here at the beach. Not a friend so much as a wing man in our endless pursuit of 'crazy bitches' as Chewy calls them. His name is Marty, and he lives next door. Marty is a contractor and lives alone in a small beach house. It was meant to be a weekend 'get away place' for his wife and him. They got divorced shortly after the house was built and it became Marty's full time get away place. She got their big house in Santa Clarita.

The beach is an eclectic place. The people you meet here include retired attorneys, building contractors, Navy Seabees, fishermen, and real estate agents. Most are either well on their way towards alcoholism or trying to recover from it. All walks of life are present and accounted for. From mega rich to barely getting by.

Nearly all my neighbors have a DUI on their record. Many have more than one. None of their stories are as good as my friend Marty's though. Shortly before I met Marty, he was out celebrating the official end of his marriage with his divorce attorney at several of our local bars. Since all our bars are close by, Marty decided to drive his golf cart for this adventure. After consuming their fill, Marty was driving the cart home with his attorney in the passenger seat. About one block from home, he was pulled over by the ever-vigilant County Sheriff. Now many of you may be thinking what I was thinking. Can you really get a DUI while driving an electric golf cart that can't go faster than 25 mph one block from your house? Well in California it turns out you can. Marty spent the night in jail, and they impounded his cart. Apparently divorce attorneys can't help much on DUI infractions. Now whenever we go out, he makes me drive the cart.

Around here the bars are arranged in what locals' think of as 'The Circuit', which is basically just a big loop encompassing the entire beach. Traditionally one starts and ends The Circuit at our local dive bar called the Ketch. The Ketch is known for its cash-only policy, its no frills drinks, and its no nonsense bartenders. But the drinks are strong and cheap. So that's where we start. Experienced patrons like ourselves know better than to order anything more complicated than a beer or a rum and Coke. I've seen

Ketch bartenders kick out women who even try to order any type of flavored vodka. Ordering any trendy cocktails like say "Sex on the Beach" can get you 86'd for life.

The Ketch opens early (long before noon) and stays open the latest of all our bars. The exact times of both are controlled by the whims of the bartenders and vary based on their mood. It's about seven PM when Marty and I wander in. Not much is happening, but many locals have already been there for hours, and the place is just getting started. We look around but it's too early for any crazy bitches. We satisfy ourselves with a few beers and a game of pool. Next stop is a local restaurant bar, The Mermaid's Tail. It's the largest such establishment on our beach with live music most nights. Here we order a few fish tacos with our beers. They have Guinness stout on tap which is my favorite. The barmaids here are friendlier and way cuter than those at the Ketch.

"I'll have a Bud Light for my friend and a Guinness for me. Make it dark and bitter like my soul."

The pretty barmaid rewards me with a few giggles and a flirty hair flip. I doubt she's ever even had a Guinness, but she handles the taps like a pro, topping the dark liquid with a perfect creamy head. I complement her for giving me just the "right amount of head". More giggles.

There are some single ladies here but they're in large groups. Experienced beach bar cruisers like Marty and I know it's best to wait until they've had a few more drinks before approaching. This place draws a classier crowd, so the likely best-case scenario for us will be to enjoy a few dances and leave with a few phone numbers. We enjoy our fish tacos and beer while waiting for the music to start.

Eventually, we leave the Mermaid's Tail after a few dances and a few phone numbers. I give all my numbers to Marty. He's got the gift of gab, and I rarely date – not in the conventional sense anyway. Dating can lead to more emotional commitment than I am willing to offer at the moment. We head out to the next stop on The Circuit called The Outlook Bar and Grill. The Outlook is only one slight step classier than the Ketch. It features a large sectional coach facing whatever entertainment might be offered that evening. Suffice to say this is not a piece of furniture you'd want anywhere near your home. Tonight, they're featuring a decent rock singer / guitarist, so Marty and I flop right down on that coach next to some rock and roll girls. We chat them up. Buy them a few beers. Then a few shots. Soon there is as much alcohol spilling onto the couch as going into the girls. Nobody cares.

Marty tries to get all three of the ladies to come back with us to his house for a nightcap and a cheese plate. Marty feels strongly that everyone should consume charcuterie after drinking heavily. He always has an amazing selection ready for unexpected female visitors. The girls are clearly tempted by our offer, but three girls and two guys are an awkward combination and eventually they politely decline.

It's getting late so it's time to complete The Circuit back at the Ketch. By now most of the single beach people who remain unattached this evening are heading back there as well. It's the final stop on The Circuit so there's a bit of desperation in the air.

Marty and I order a nice single malt and go out onto the bar patio to smoke cigars. It's been a fun night. We met lots of fun people, had a few laughs, and nobody got a DUI.

Marty is very careful about driving these days. Not careful enough to stop drinking of course. He's just more careful about being caught. And for good reason. Now, even as a passenger in a vehicle being driven under the influence, he could lose his license indefinitely. Between bar stops he makes me pull off the road and drive the golf cart stealthily in dark parking lots and alleyways. If we see another vehicle on the street, we pull up behind the nearest tree. All this is unnecessary of course. My capacity for alcohol consumption is legendary. I suspect some of my supernatural abilities have migrated to my liver. I barely feel a buzz from a night of drinking. Sometimes I wonder why I bother drinking at all.

Such is not at all the case for the lovely young lady who wanders out to join us on the patio. She's clearly not capable of piloting a moving vehicle, but I suspect she has other talents that are still very much intact. After a quick hello, she sits down and joins our conversation. We soon discover that her name is Lisa and she's had a hell of day doing job interviews. Turns out Lisa is an exotic dancer and she's hoping to do that again now that she's recently divorced. Today's interviews did not go as she had hoped. Lisa is attractive, but now she's in her late thirties which is almost retirement age in her profession. Of course, Marty and I give her plenty of reassurance, complimenting her various features and body parts. As if to confirm our opinion, Lisa gives us an occasional up-close glimpse of these areas.

I'm intrigued by Lisa's bubbly personality and lack of modesty. That's always a killer combination for me. I invite her to play a game of pool. She says she's going to kick my ass. I tell her if she loses, I'm going to spank hers. Her interest in me suddenly perks up a bit. We end up playing a very sexy game of pool where both of us try to distract the other while shooting. When it's her turn, I come up behind her and dry hump her while she is bent over. Then when it's my turn she does the same while giving my cock a quick squeeze. She's not bad at pool, but I'm less intoxicated and beat her easily.

"So how do you want your spanking? Over my knee or tied to my bed?"

"Both sound yummy. I'll let you know."

The Ketch bartender has just announced last call. Marty invites both of us back to his house for some good tequila and charcuterie. Lisa looks at me funny, so I translate Marty-speak for her. "He means a cheese plate with cold cuts. It's actually quite good."

Marty gives Lisa a horsey back ride all the way to his house. She's making cute "Yaaaaa Hooooo!" noises the whole way. I like her. Lisa has a fun wild side that's clearly on display tonight. She's not the kind of girl I'd typically go for, but variety is indeed the spice of life. Her free spirit is also on display all the way down her right arm which is covered with colorful tattoo flowers and vines. My friend Tom would hate that (more on him later) but I find it intriguing. Maybe I can examine her more closely later for other more intimate body art.

Once at Marty's we have a few shots of fine Don Julio and chow down on his charcuterie. Both are excellent and Lisa partakes of both rather vigorously. She sits herself down on Marty's kitchen island making herself the center of our attention. Normally Marty would frown on such behavior - he's very territorial when it comes to his kitchen. Tonight, he seems a bit more relaxed. I guess getting a DUI while driving your golf cart helps put things into perspective a bit.

Anyway, as Lisa is clearly positioned for fun, I walk over to her. She's exactly at eye level and looks very kissable. So, I kiss the girl. She kisses back hard while rubbing herself against me.

"That was fun but I'm still going to spank you later."

"But I haven't told you my choice of position yet."

"We might have to try it both ways to see which we like better."

Lisa gives me a sexy pout that tells me all I need to know about her preferences in that area.

Marty starts making yawning sounds which I know from experience means he's done for the night and wants us to leave. I offer to drive Lisa home, but she prefers to see where I live first. That's fine with me so we walk on over.

My house is one of the most historic on the beach and dates back to the 1920's. Local legend has it that back in the day Hollywood stars like Clark Gable, Carole Lombard, and Errol Flynn partied at my house. Later the house briefly became a local brothel. It definitely has a strong sex vibe.

A vibe that Lisa is also feeling at the moment it seems. We've hardly made it inside before she starts kissing me. I guide her to the couch so we can explore each other more thoroughly. She catches her breath and asks when the spanking starts. Without a word, I roll her over my knee and pull down her tight jeans. She's wearing sexy thongs and has great tan lines. Gotta love those stripper girls.

After satisfying her immediate needs, I take her up to bed. There we explore most of her kinky side and just a little bit of my own.

By morning she's calling me "sir" a lot and she is sore in all the right places. I'm pleased to see she is all happy and glowing with a definite sparkle in her eyes. I drive her home feeling good that I had turned her bad day into a fun night. It's kind of a public service really. Perhaps not as fulfilling as saving people from hurricanes, but a lot less stressful.

I find myself wondering what Jennifer would think of my new lifestyle at the beach. Turns out I don't have to wait long to find out. I take a quick peek into the future before breakfast and notice the following headline, clearly from Jennifer: **High Five Doodle Boy - Just Save Those Fuzzy Red Handcuffs for Me.** She used to call me that to annoy me, but now it makes me smile.

> The West coast has the sunshine,
> And the girls all get so tanned.
> - California Girls by Mike Love / Brian Wilson

# 3
# THE SHOEMAKER GIRLS

Ever since I moved across country trading South Florida beaches for those in California, I've been lobbying my friends to come visit. Finally, someone did, my old friend Tom from Miami. Tom is a not only a good friend but also my former work buddy at the National Hurricane Center. Without doubt, he is a brilliant mathematician and physicist. But what I find most interesting about Tom are his dating habits.

Tom dates like the rest of us pursue our careers. In other words, he dates like it's his job. Like his real career in mathematics, Tom's approach to dating has strict rules and methods. His rules are a rather specific and lengthy list of the attributes that potential dates must and must not have. His methods tend to gravitate towards the technical and efficient – computer dating and speed dating being two examples. Tom is the most efficient dater I've ever seen. It seems like every week he meets a new potential ex-girlfriend. Tom is as efficient at vetting and rejecting women as he is in meeting them in the first place. His inventory turn of women is rapid. Tom averages about four new ex-girlfriends a month. His entire relationship lifecycle, from meet and greet to breakup, averages about six weeks. Those are actual statistics. Tom tracks his dating numbers. Even when I was living in Miami, his girlfriends rarely lasted long enough for me to meet them – proving that he is just as efficient at ending relationships as he is in starting them up. For Tom, dating is all about managing the flow of women through his dating pipeline. At his current rate of consumption, Tom estimates that he will have exhausted the entire eligible pool of available Miami females within the next three years. It may not be romantic, but you do have to admire the efficiency of the process.

Tom has so many ex-girlfriends that he assigns them nicknames so we can discuss them later. Usually, the nickname memorializes some defining characteristic of the girl to help us all remember them. The list includes such memorable names as Hammer Toes, Tattoo Girl, The Jackhammer, Psycho, and The Bushwhacker.

I lured Tom out here with the promise of meeting lots of new single women that he hasn't vetted yet. In truth, the vast majority of women here would not meet his criteria, but I didn't tell him that. The biggest problem is his "no tattoo" rule. He's very strict about this and almost every woman here at the beach has more than one of them. Fortunately, many of these women have their tattoos in places that Tom won't immediately look. Since he's only out here for a week, my theory is that won't be enough time for him to notice the problem.

I failed to anticipate two very real problems with this theory. The first problem is that beach girls often wear skimpy bikinis. Even when they're not on the beach, you can still see most of them through their equally skimpy cover-ups. There's almost no place for a tattoo to hide.

The second problem is the interview. I forgot that when Tom meets a new potential ex-girlfriend, he interviews them. It's almost like a job interview. He can find out more about their history and background in five minutes that I would in a week. Somewhere in his interview questionnaire is always the question, "So do you have any interesting tattoos?" Crap.

Tom: How come every woman we meet in this town has tatts?

Me: I don't know, maybe because it's a beach town?

Tom: That's unfortunate. Some of them are hot.

Me: Maybe we could temporarily suspend the tattoo rule while you're here.

Tom: I would if I could.

So, Tom and I go off in search of more beach adventures. Hunting ink virgins as Tom puts it. Our first stop is to visit my newly acquired sailboat which is docked near my house. It's a thirty-six-foot Hunter with all the bells and whistles. Today is not a great sailing day, so I suggest we just go aboard and have a few beers. As we're walking to the boat, we encounter two lovely ladies heading our way. And they have questions.

One of them is tall and dark skinned. The other is shorter with dark hair. Both are attractive and neither has any obvious body art.

Tall Dark Girl: Do you guys know where there might be some music around here? We're visiting from out of town.

She has a very classy English accent, so I'm immediately intrigued. Tom seems more focused on her friend.

Me: There's a band playing later at the Mermaids Tail down the street. But right now, Tom and I are about to fire up some music and cold beers on my sailboat. Care to join us?

The girls exchange looks. I don't speak Girl Body Language, but I'm getting a positive vibe.

Tall Dark Girl: Is there tequila?

Me: Yep. My boat is called Margaritaville. We're fully stocked with Don Julio.

I'm not sure the girls know Don Julio from Jose Cuervo, but we had them at tequila. The four of us head over to Margaritaville for what's known in these parts as a dock party. Soon the tequila shots are flowing, and the Jimmy Buffet music is blasting.

Tall Dark Girl's name is Emily. Her friend is Tracey. Emily is from Brighton Beach in the UK. She's visiting her friend Tracey for the summer. Tracey lives in Bakersfield which is about 100 miles further inland and fifty degrees hotter than here. I tell them they've made a very wise decision to visit our beach. Our weather is way better and so is our entertainment.

And right now, Tom and I are their entertainment.

I take Emily down into the salon berths and show her around. Tom is interviewing Tracey out on the main deck. My interview method is a bit different and less verbal. Soon Emily and I are making out like crazy in the main berth. She's wearing a short sun dress that highlights her crazy long legs. I'm totally enjoying the view. I challenge her to a game of tequila body shots. The objective is to find the most creative ways to spill tequila all over yourselves and then have the other person lick it up. Turns out I'm pretty creative.

After making a serious dent in my tequila supply, Tom and I walk the girls back to their weekend rental apartment and make plans for the evening. Tom hasn't found any deal breakers yet with Tracey and I'm rather smitten with Emily. She's bright, sexy, and tons of fun. Plus, there's that accent and those legs. Killer combo. We make plans to pick the girls up for an early dinner at the Mermaid's Tail. My favorite local band, The Shoemaker Brothers, will be playing tonight. These guys are crazy good, and I tell everyone they're in for a treat.

It's a fine summer night at the beach and we walk to dinner. The girls have transformed themselves from casual sexy beachwear to elegant sexy evening wear. Emily is wearing a long, tight red dress that accents her curves with a slit to expose those long, lovely legs. It's that semitransparent clingy material that Jennifer used to wear sometimes. With that thought comes the all too familiar pang of pain somewhere in my gut. I drive away that painful memory by making a remark that Emily would probably call "cheeky".

Me: So, Emily, can we assume your bra matches that dress?

Emily: You Americans are so cheeky. What kind of a question is that to ask a lady?

Me: I guess I shouldn't ask about your knickers then?

Emily gives me a devilish grin and flashes her sexy red panties at me.

Emily: Does that satisfy your curiosity about my undergarments?

Me: For now. I'll probably have more questions later.

Dinner at the Mermaid's Tail is hardly fine dining – fish tacos, burgers, and beer. But we're all having a great time, and no one is complaining. The Shoemaker Brothers take the stage with their unique mix of blues, ballads, and rock. Most of the crowd are already big fans and they even have a few groupies that follow them everywhere. I can tell that Emily and Tracey are intrigued. We take them over to the dance floor, and both girls are flirting up a storm with the band.

In hindsight it was not my best idea to introduce them to the Brothers during their break. I was just showing off the fact that I was tight with some real up and coming musicians. What I failed to consider was that these particular musicians are also world class horn-dogs. Within mere seconds, the Brothers had secured both girls' numbers and had arranged future dates.

Tom: What just happened?

Me: The Shoemaker Brothers stole our women.

Tom: Maybe you should put that on t-shirts and sell them.

Me: It would only encourage them.

We teased the girls about becoming Shoemaker groupies and laughed it off, but it put a bit of a lid on our expectations for the evening. Especially since both Emily and Tracey could not stop talking about how cute and talented the band members all were. In fairness, I guess they had a point particularly compared to weather geeks like Tom and myself.

We dropped the girls back at their place and walked back to Margaritaville to smoke cigars and sample a bit of single malt.

"I think Tracey and I had a real connection tonight. She wants me to call her sometime."

"Tom, you live across the country from her, how's that going to work?"

"Maybe you're right. I thought she had potential though. What did you think of Emily?"

"She's okay. She says she wants to get together with us for breakfast tomorrow. I told her I'd call her in the morning. Not sure whether I really want to though."

"Why not? Do you have something better planned?"

"Not really. I just can't help comparing the girls I meet here to Jennifer. They never seem to measure up."

"Dude you're going to have to stop doing that or you'll never meet anyone. No one is going to live up to that standard."

"Are you seriously giving me dating advice? You're the guy with all those arbitrary and unbreakable dating criteria remember? No one lives up to your standards either."

"They're not arbitrary, those rules have been carefully refined and perfected after many years of actual dating experience!"

"Sounds to me like you just listed a few characteristics of all your worst relationships. You can't tell me those criteria are in any way scientific."

"Hey, I ran a regression analysis on them. All those characteristics are highly correlated with short, unpleasant relationships."

Listen up girls, this is why you should never date a mathematician. Or a guy still in love with his angelic ex-girlfriend for that matter.

"I'm thinking we should give these girls a nickname."
"How about The Shoemaker Girls?"
"Sounds about right."

The next morning, we do in fact take the girls to breakfast. We have a local diner on the beach that serves some of the best breakfast dishes anywhere. All my beach rat friends hang there. What we intended to be a table for four turns out to be a table for ten as many of those friends want to join us. Everyone is curious about the new girls. Seems to be an unfortunate trend.

This time we manage to pry the girls away and herd them off to the beach. Both are wearing skimpy bikinis under their shorts and tops. Emily's is a particularly fetching shade of bright yellow, contrasting nicely with her dark skin and floppy beach hat. As we lay on her blanket, she tells me about growing up in England and how much she's loving California. She's charming and fun. I can tell Tom is having a good time with Tracey as well – so far, no tattoos in sight.

After a bit of amorous beach play, we take the girls back to my house. It has a two-story bar as you walk in, so perfect for entertaining. The bar is fully stocked and even has a frozen margarita machine which everyone wants to try after being in the sun all afternoon. I make up a few batches of my favorite beach cocktail and we all start to get a bit rowdy as Emily likes to say.

Eventually we move from rowdy, to cheeky, to scandalous. I walk Emily upstairs to my bedroom while Tom continues to entertain Tracey on the couch. I bring a bottle of fine tequila upstairs as well, because as we all know, tequila makes your clothes fall off. Lying Emily down on my bed, she enjoys a great view of the harbor while I enjoy a great view of her. I tell her I'm going to lick that tequila off every inch of her. I start with those long sexy legs, toes first. By the time I get back up to her lips, she's pretty damn rowdy and my head is starting to spin from all the tequila. Time to let her catch up.

Lying down on the bed, I tell her to "do me". Turns out that Emily follows directions extremely well. I keep telling her she "missed a spot" and she obediently goes back for a redo. Pretty soon, she'd licked off as much tequila on me as I had on her. In addition to being crazy fun, her tongue massage had the added benefits of letting my head clear a bit and making me rock hard for her. Putting those two benefits together, I rolled her over on her back and spread those amazing legs of hers skyward. I put the hardest part of me next to the wettest part of her and stared down at her smiling. Waiting. Finally, I hear her softly whisper "please", so I give her what she wants most at this moment. I bet she isn't thinking about those stupid Shoemaker Brothers anymore!

Yes, I really am that petty.

But competition brings out the best performances and Emily was expressing her appreciation rather loudly. In sharp contrast with her normal, refined British demeanor, Emily screamed out the most amazing collection of dirty talk I've ever encountered. I didn't catch all of it, but there were emphatic and repeated references to words like "CUNT! COCK! POUND! SLAP! ASS! TITS! CHOKE! HARD! HARDER! BITCH! MAKE ME! SLUT! YOURS! and the ever-popular WHORE!" After I'd tried just about every position I could think of, we both finally had enough. I roll off her, completely exhausted and totally satisfied. From the expression on her face – glazed eyes, very mussed up hair, and a slight smile – I think Emily feels about the same. Later she confirmed this by whispering in my ear, "I really needed that, you shagged the fuck out of me. THANK YOU!" So polite these British girls.

Later after we walked the girls back home, Tom was feeling chatty.

"I've got to say, you've got a pretty good life out here on the beach. I'm sorry I need to leave tomorrow."

"Stay as long as you like. It'll take you at least a month or two to meet all the single women out here."

"I wish. But I am definitely going to plan a return visit. In the meantime, Tracey wants to come visit me in Miami."

"Are you going to keep in touch with her?"

"Of course. I need to complete her vetting. It's looking good so far. Are you going to see Emily again?"

"I doubt it. She's going back to England in a few weeks. And you know how it is with women. The first encounter is always the best. After that, you're just trying in vain to capture the passion of the first time."

"And I thought I was cynical. You don't really believe that."

"These days I do. Ever since Jennifer left."

Tom didn't have a response to that. Sadly, neither do I.

> There's a man who leads a life of danger,
> To everyone he meets he stays a stranger,
> With every move he makes another chance he takes,
> Odds are he won't live to see tomorrow.
> - Secret Agent Man by Johnny Rivers

# 4
# SPECIAL AGENT TOOMEY

I'm Special Agent Nathan Toomey, FBI. I head up a secret program within the Bureau called the Paranormal Investigation Service. It's not really secret, we just don't talk about it much. Our mission is to investigate situations where crimes are being committed using what appear to be paranormal methods – those that are beyond the scope of normal scientific understanding. Often these crimes turn out to have more ordinary explanations where very clever individuals make things appear to be paranormal in nature. For example, if a criminal version of David Copperfield decided to rob banks by making all the money in the vault disappear, that case would likely wind up on my desk. My team has special expertise in the ways of magic tricks and deception that ordinary agents would not have. We can usually spot such things quite easily because we know what to look for. But not always.

Take one of my current cases for example, the strange and twisted story of Jake Hedley. The case was first brought to my attention by our Paranormal Alert Team. The function of that team is to monitor world events for signs of any paranormal activity. This is how we find and recruit people with special abilities into our organization. The team noticed that over the past year, the National Hurricane Center (NHC) in Miami had suddenly and inexplicably increased their hurricane forecasting accuracy by a factor of ten. Our analysts further noted that this level of accuracy had continued over the entire mid-Atlantic hurricane season and was nearly a statistical impossibility. The odds of this happening by random chance were over one thousand to one.

I decided this situation warranted further investigation and opened a case file. Our first step was to gather intelligence about the inner workings of the NHC. We set up surveillance of their hurricane forecasting group personnel and tapped their computers. Nothing out of the ordinary happened until the start of the new hurricane season. Twelve days before the first hurricane of the season formed, we noticed some unusual computer runs involving the Hurricane Center's premier hurricane forecasting model, the American Global Forecasting system known as AGF. These runs were not scheduled as part of the normal hurricane tracking and forecasting process. The run logs recorded them as routine maintenance updates, but we could find no record of any authorized maintenance activity.

We intensified our surveillance to record all computer activity by the users and workstations involved in the suspicious computer runs. That's when things started to get interesting. Twelve days before the second hurricane of the new season formed, we discovered another unusual AGF computer run in the middle of the night. This time we uncovered the exact nature of that run. Turns out that the run was initiated from the workstation of Mr. Philip Thorsen, the head of the NHC's computer forecasting group. While it is not at all unusual for Mr. Thorsen to schedule such AGF runs, the nature of this one was very unusual. Our tap on Mr. Thorson's workstation revealed that he activated a previously unknown data entry module of the AGF system and entered some highly suspicious data. The data appeared to contain details of a hurricane's formation twelve days in the future. Sure enough, a hurricane did form twelve days later exactly as Mr. Thorsen's data predicted.

Shortly before this computer run, we intercepted a phone call originating from Mr. Thorsen's cell phone. The call was made to a former NHC colleague of Mr. Thorsen, a man named Jake Hedley. Mr. Hedley had been one of the lead forecasting analysts at NHC and had worked closely with Mr. Thorsen. Six months ago, Mr. Hedley suddenly resigned from NHC stating personal reasons and is now living in Southern California. He is currently working as a delivery driver for Amazon.

While none of that is particularly unusual - a middle-aged man experiencing a midlife crisis, quitting his job, and moving to the beach is practically cliché – the nature of the phone call definitely was unusual. Here is the recorded transcript:

Mr. Thorsen: Hey Jake, its Phil. What's happening at the beach these days?
Mr. Hedley: Not much. Just making the world a better place by delivering packages and chasing around those beach girls. How about you?
Mr. Thorsen: Any word from Jennifer?
Mr. Hedley: Not lately. I think she's gone for good.
Mr. Thorsen: Sorry to hear that buddy. Whatcha have for me today?
Mr. Hedley: Just checked the Mega Event Stream. Looks like you'll have another hurricane forming near the Bahamas in twelve days. Hurricane Becky. Doesn't look too bad though.
Mr. Thorsen: Okay, let me grab a pen.

The rest of the call involved Mr. Hedley giving Mr. Thorsen detailed information about Hurricane Becky's formation including the exact location, wind speed, time, and barometric pressure. Later analysis proved these details to be exactly correct.

We did some checking on the woman Mr. Hedley mentions during the call. Her name is Jennifer Ortega. She was his live-in girlfriend prior to his departure from NHC. She mysteriously dropped off the grid around the same time Mr. Hedley resigned his position and moved to California. There has been no missing person's report filed by her family or anyone else. We're still trying to locate her.

We also have no idea what Mr. Hedley meant by "checking his Mega Event Stream". We ran that term by our team of scientists and paranormal investigators, but no one had heard of such a thing. A routine Google search came up empty. One of our physicists speculated the term might have to do with the passage of events through time, whatever that means.

Even if it turns out that Ms. Ortega is alive and well with no foul play involved, we have enough evidence in this case to bring Federal charges against both Mr. Thorsen and Mr. Hedley. The ADF computer model is a federally funded asset and is therefore Federal property. Conspiracy to alter or destroy federal property is a felony.

Our real interest in this case is not to enforce federal property laws. We need to understand how Mr. Hedley can see twelve days into the future. That's a talent the government could use in more ways than just hurricane prediction. I intend to use whatever means are necessary to find the truth here and, if possible, persuade Mr. Hedley to broaden the use of his powers in the interests of the US Government.

Now that we have sufficient probable cause, we've begun comprehensive surveillance of all Mr. Hedley's activity. So far, we haven't uncovered anything illegal or supernatural. Just a bunch of short encounters with women living close by. He had a recent visit from another of his colleagues at the NHC but all they did was talk about dating and the women they were meeting. There was nothing about hurricane predictions or future events. Mr. Hedley seems to have traded his promising career at NHC for a life of debauchery at the beach. Whenever he's not actually having sex, he's either talking about it or actively trying to have it. His ex-girlfriend Jennifer keeps coming up in conversation, but so far as we know, he's had no contact with her. He tells his friends that he misses her but makes absolutely no attempt to find her. None of us know what to make of that.

One other odd thing we've noticed during our surveillance of Mr. Hedley is that he often talks to his dog. And not just like regular people do. Mr. Hedley talks to the dog like he's having an entire conversation with someone, except there's only one person talking. The dog doesn't even bark. At first, we thought Mr. Hedley was just talking to himself, but then our spotters on the ground got pictures and it turns our Mr. Hedley does have a dog – a Golden Doodle he calls 'Chewy'. We're getting transcripts of those conversations, but so far it appears they are mostly about this Jennifer woman and something about Chewy's missing balls. None of our analysts know what to make of that either, but we're bringing in some canine experts.

We are going to continue our surveillance activity, but given the lack of progress, it looks like we're going to have to confront him with what we know. Squeeze him a little and see what happens - for the good of the country.

> Listen, hotshot. I'm gonna tell you something right now.
> I don't care for you or for the putrid sludge you're troweling out.
> - Detective Joe Friday, Dragnet

# 5
# A PISSING CONTEST

An odd thing happened today. I was taking my regular peek at upcoming events, and I noticed something unusual. At first, I thought it might have been another one of those cute little messages from Jennifer, but this one had a more ominous tone: **JAKE IS CONFRONTED BY A PISS AGENT.**

I have no idea what a PISS Agent might be, but it doesn't sound good. There were no underlying details listed for this event, but it's supposed to happen today. One thing for sure, if someone knocks on my door today, I'm going to keep my distance. I mean beach life is crazy sometimes, but so far no one has tried to pee on me – maybe a little squirting occasionally, but usually I can get out of the way and my sheets are washable. Forewarned is forearmed as they say.

Sure enough, at exactly the appointed time, I get a knock on my door. It's a guy wearing a suit and tie. One thing I've learned living at the beach is that absolutely nobody wears a suit and tie. The most formal attire I've ever seen around here has been a silk Tommy Bahama shirt. I know immediately I'm in some kind of trouble.

Plus, this guy looks like he just stepped out from an episode of Dragnet. Dark suit. Dark tie. Close cropped haircut. No facial hair. Dark Ray Bans. Yeah, I'm totally fucked. I open the door and prepare for the worst – making sure I keep out of pee range.

He flashes his badge, which is almost unnecessary at this point.

"FBI. Special Agent Toomey. Are you Jake Hedley?"
"Guilty. I mean yes."
"I need to ask you a few questions. Can I come in?"
"Okay. The bathroom's over there."
"I think we should just talk in the living room."
"That's fine, have a seat."

I direct him toward the plastic chair closest to the bathroom. I stay out of range on the couch.

"Let me get right to the point Mr. Hedley. My team at the FBI has been looking into your activities for a while now. We've discovered some very disturbing things."

"And what team would that be exactly Agent Toomey?"

Agent Toomey pushes his card at me across the coffee table. It seems okay so I pick it up.

"That's *Special* Agent Toomey. I head up the Bureau's Paranormal Investigation Service. We investigate crimes that have unnatural causes."

"Your card says you're Special Agent Nathan Toomey from the Paranormal Investigation Service."

"That's right."

"So essentially, you're a PIS agent then?"

"We prefer not to use that acronym."

"Well then, I guess it's safe to say you probably never use the acronym for your full title, Paranormal Investigation Service Special Agent Nathan Toomey. Am I correct?"

"You do realize I have a gun, right?"

"Just a little beach levity. You know I could have gone with "The Man from PIS" but I was holding back. So, what 'disturbing things' are we talking here Special Agent Toomey? Am I over my limit for banging beach babes?"

"No but if there was a limit for that, you'd probably be in violation. There is one woman in particular that I would like to ask you about. What do you know about the whereabouts of your ex-girlfriend Jennifer Ortega?"

"Nothing actually. I lost track of her when she moved out of my house in Miami. We haven't talked since."

"Why did she leave?"

"She said she couldn't be with me any longer. Something about my job, as I recall. Anyway, she told me she couldn't see me anymore and not to try to find her. So I didn't."

"Have you talked to her parents? No one has seen her since she left you."

"No, I haven't but I suspect you already know that."

"You don't seem surprised that she's missing."

"In order to be missing, there has to be someone trying to find you. Is anyone trying to find her? Has anyone filed a missing person's report? Didn't she notify her school and her family that she was leaving?"

"It seems you know a lot about her disappearance after all Mr. Hedley. Anything else you'd care to share?"

"Jennifer told me she needed to get away, far away, from me. I guess she did."

"Did you have a fight with her when she told you she was leaving you?"

"No not at all. I love Jennifer, and I understood her reasons for going away."

"You don't think it's odd that someone you love can suddenly disappear without a trace and that no one seems to know where?"

"I guess that might be a bit unusual, but it seems pretty far outside the purview of the paranormal. I mean unless you think someone turned her into a frog or something."

"If that were the only unusual thing connected with you Mr. Hedley, we wouldn't be having this conversation. What do you know about the sudden increase in hurricane forecast accuracy that the NHC was able to achieve last year?"

"I know that we improved our ability to predict hurricanes before they form. I participated in a research mission to do just that. We discovered the precise conditions necessary for their formation. That led to an exponential increase in forecast accuracy."

"That increase in hurricane forecasting accuracy is mathematically impossible - as I'm sure you already know Mr. Hedley."

Chewy comes sauntering into the room fresh from his morning nap. Hardly a watch dog that one.

Chewy: Who is this guy? He looks like he's dressed for a mob funeral. I don't like the way he smells.

"This must be your dog, Chewy."

"Chewy, meet Special Agent Nathan Toomey from the Paranormal Investigation Service, FBI."

Chewy: Did you already call him PISSANT?

"Pretty much. Nice to know I'm not the only one who thinks of these things."

"Thinks of what things?"

"Sorry, just talking to my dog. He doesn't care for your smell by the way."

"So how do you explain being able to do the statistically impossible with your hurricane forecasts?"

"Maybe I'm just a really good guesser."

"Or maybe you can see the future."

"Wouldn't that be even more statistically impossible, Special Agent Toomey?"

"In my experience, no. I've met many people with uncanny insight and unexplained capabilities. Nothing like yours though. Look, cut the bullshit Hedley. We know about your secret backdoor. We have you on tape feeding future hurricane data to your buddy Thorsen over at NHC. Now tell me what's really going on here or I'm going to bring Federal charges against you and your friend."

"Is being really good at predicting hurricanes a federal crime these days?"

"It is when you conspire to create a secret backdoor to a multimillion-dollar federal computer asset. I've got enough evidence to put you both away for twenty years, minimum."

Chewy: Looks like you're fucked buddy. What's he mean by "put you away?" Is that like when you lock me in my crate? Who's going to feed me?

"Why do you always have to make everything about you?"
"How is this about me?"
"Once again, talking to my dog. He was worried about who's going to feed him. WHILE I'M IN JAIL FOR TWENTY FUCKING YEARS!"
"Wait, you can see the future AND talk to your dog?"
"Everybody can talk to their dog. This ungrateful creature talks to me."
"I didn't hear anything."
"I'm the only one who can hear him."
"Do all dogs talk to you? What about cats?"
"No, just Chewy. Plus, nobody cares what cats have to say."

Chewy: That's true. Cats are boring.

"Are you going to tell me about this future vision thing of yours or do we have to go downtown? And what's wrong with your eye? It looked like you were having a stroke there for a second."

"Downtown? Really? We barely have a decent restaurant around here. We're hours away from anything resembling a downtown. You really need a new shtick Toomey."

"Alright, down to the station then. That work for you? Spill it Hedley."

"No big deal. I can see twelve minutes into the future. Yours, mine, or anyone's."

"Prove it."

"I knew you were going to say that – even without looking ahead. Here's what else I know Toomey. In five minutes, your cell is going to ring. It's your wife, Lisa. Normally you wouldn't answer but now you will because I told you it would happen. Lisa is pissed because you forgot to put gas in her car when you went out to play cards with the boys. By the way, Lisa knows you actually went to see your stripper friend, Tiffany, but she's waiting to spring that on you later. Before you can tell her anything, she's going to hang up on you. By the way, Tiffany is right now leaving you a text message that will arrive just after Lisa hangs up. She misses your cock."

"Listen hotshot, I don't care for that putrid sludge you're troweling out... But just in case you're not entirely full of shit, is Lisa going to believe me if I tell her I don't know anyone named Tiffany?"

"I doubt it. She saw the text message you sent to Tiffany before you left for your flight here. Texting your stripper girlfriend that you want to fuck her in the ass tends to leave quite an impression on wives as I understand. By the way, how do you get to be a Special Agent for the FBI and not set a password on your phone?"

Agent Toomey is looking very uncomfortable now. When his phone rings, he looks like he going to faint. I hear yelling on the other end, then silence. Almost immediately he gets the familiar ping of an incoming text message. Seeing his cheeks redden, I can tell it's from Tiffany.

"So now do you understand why you don't want to fuck with me, Special Agent Toomey? I can fuck you up in ways you could never even imagine. You won't even know what happened. Now do you want to tell me what you really want from me?"

"Can't you just look into the future and see?"

"I already did, but it's more fun to hear it from you directly."

"I'm based in Chicago. There's been a lot of terrorism activity lately in and around the city. My group sometimes uses people with talents like yours to help us find the bad guys. We know there are several terrorist cells operating in our area, but we haven't been able to uncover anything solid yet. These guys are smart and are wise to our normal methods. That's why we need to use abnormal methods. Like you."

"You law enforcement people are all the same. You always think you need to threaten and intimidate in order to get what you want. Did it ever occur to you that I might want to help out? Chicago is my hometown. I'm not happy to hear it's now a terrorist target."

"Okay point taken. No more intimidation. How do you think you can help us? No offense, but a twelve-minute glimpse into the future is not enough time to do much."

"It was enough to fuck you up pretty good wasn't it? Imagine what I could do to someone that I really didn't like. Besides, I have a few other talents that might come in handy."

"So, you'll help us then?"

"Assuming you don't do anything stupid like trying to pressure me or my friends again, then yes. And for Christ's sake Toomey, get yourself another name for your group. I can't be the only one that shortened your title to PISSANT. Even my dog figured it out."

And that's how I began working for the FBI's newest investigative unit – the Unexplained Phenomenon Investigation Service. I can only hope they're better at catching bad guys than they are at naming things.

No one likes us. I don't know why,
We may not be perfect, but heaven knows we try,
But all around, even our old friends put us down,
Let's drop the big one and see what happens.
 - Political Science by Randy Newman

# 6
# THE BIG ONE

I briefed Special Agent Toomey, giving him a few more details about my special abilities to see the future. I told him about the Mega Event Streams and how I can see major world events twelve *days* into the future. I didn't mention that I can also sometimes change those events. That's something I'm going to keep to myself for now. People who put too much trust in the Government often get burned. You don't need to see the future in order to know that.

So now I check my Mega Event Streams every day. If I see a hurricane coming, I call Phil. If I see something related to a major crime or terrorism, I call Toomey. So far, it's all been quiet.

Special Agent Toomey invited me to attend an FBI terrorist seminar last week being given to the LAPD. He felt I'd be able to help more if I understood more about terrorist cells and tactics. I did learn some things about that, but mostly I learned a bunch of arcane FBI jargon. Things like UNSUB. That stands for "Unidentified Subject", referring to the unknown person or persons that commit a particular crime. I asked why they didn't just call it UNSUS, for "Unidentified Suspect" but they just told me that a suspect in law enforcement lingo means something different. A suspect to them is an actual identified person they think may be involved in a crime. Whereas "Subject" is a more vague term meaning anyone being investigated in a criminal matter – whether identified or not. Personally, I think they're just splitting hairs because UNSUB makes a better acronym but whatever.

I did learn a few useful things at the terrorist seminar. Most of them were disturbing. It turns out we have many active terrorist cells operating in the US these days. Some are involved in international terrorism like al-Qaeda. Some are domestic terrorist groups, either on the left, right, or single issue (for example animal rights, abortion, and environment.) All seek to disrupt and destroy the existing order through fear and intimidation. Agent Toomey is focused on the international ones – particularly those operating out of the Chicago area where he is based. His sources, both paranormal and otherwise, are showing a big uptick in terror group activity there. Some of that activity is picked up through SIGINT – intelligence agency speak for Signals Intelligence which includes all sorts of electronic communication. The US has the world's most extensive communication monitoring capability, but these days much of the nefarious kind is highly encrypted and sources are difficult to pinpoint. Even when the actual content and source of terrorist communication is unknown, however, intelligence agencies can monitor the intensity of suspicious communications in order to predict where and when a terrorist attack may occur. Recently Chicago has been abuzz with suspicious communication activity. Agent Toomey is worried.

After returning home, I had a chat with Agent Toomey about some of the disturbing details only briefly covered during the seminar. He agreed that I needed more background on the Chicago situation in order to be effective. In typical FBI fashion, they sent me a classified five-hundred-page briefing document, with all the appropriate redactions given my limited security clearance. It was a tough read, but I learned what I needed to know.

Based on the types of communications and other intelligence being gathered, intelligence agencies like the FBI can approximate what types of activities are being conducted by these terrorism cells. Typically, there are four phases of operational terror cell activity: Recruitment, Preliminary Organization & Planning, Preparatory Conduct, and Terrorist Action. Many of the cells of interest in Chicago are in the Preparatory Conduct stage, meaning they have already recruited their members, organized their cells, and selected potential targets. Now they are actively procuring the resources they need (explosives, funding, ID's, and weapons) to actually conduct a terrorist operation.

On average it takes two to three months for a terror organization like al-Qaeda to prepare an attack once their cells are in place. About one half of terror attacks occur within 30 miles of the terror cell planning location. Based on what the FBI and other intelligence agencies have learned so far, Toomey believes the attack will occur somewhere near downtown Chicago within six to ten weeks from now.

Agent Toomey recruited me in hopes that I might be able to pinpoint the actual terrorist action in terms of the type of attack, as well as the exact time and location using my ability to see the future. He thinks of me as the ultimate in SIGINT. So far nothing has shown up on my Mega Event radar so we should be safe for at least the next twelve days.

When the terrorist attack does show up in my future headlines, I'll need to make a critical decision. At the very least, I'll pass along the details of the event to Agent Toomey, but I may be able to do more. If the future event turns out to be something catastrophic, I may be able to change it to something less terrible. I've done this a few times with tropical hurricanes, but never for anything caused by man. My ability to *change* the future is far less reliable than my ability to *see* the future. I could end up making things worse or simply changing who lives and who dies. So, changing the future will only be a last resort if all else fails.

There is another thing that has the intelligence agencies (and now me) concerned. There are indications that the attack being planned on Chicago is nuclear in nature. Two years ago, as the Chicago cells were in the early formation process, international intelligence agencies uncovered a rather alarming tidbit from one mid-level al Qaeda operative who was undergoing "enhanced" interrogation. The line of questioning involved his participation in planning what is known as a "dirty bomb" attack on a western country – presumably, the US. It is well known that al Qaeda has long been researching the feasibility of such an attack.

A dirty bomb uses highly radioactive materials which are not suitable for conventional nuclear weapons, but which are readily available – such things as cesium-137, a radioactive isotope that is commonly used in medical devices. Properly distributed, using conventional explosive devices with ideal wind conditions, it is estimated that just over an ounce of the stuff would make an area the size of Manhattan virtually uninhabitable for 30 years.

One such source of cesium-137 is a medical device called an irradiator, which is used to sterilize blood and tissue samples. A typical medical irradiator contains twice the cesum-137 necessary for that hypothetical Manhattan dirty bomb. An accidental breach of the radioactive containment vessel on such a device in Seattle a few years back, caused several workers and first responders to come down with radiation sickness and made most of the six-story building in which it was housed uninhabitable to this day.

Under intense interrogation, the al Qaeda operator admitted that his superiors had lately changed their thinking about a dirty bomb attack. Turns out, such an attack doesn't fit well with al Qaeda's overall strategy. Too much risk and not enough potential damage. The problems with a dirty bomb from a terrorist point of view are twofold. First, it doesn't really kill many people – at least not right away. Second, since such a device has never been tested, no one really knows the best way to design a bomb that would spread the radioactive material over the largest possible area. Al Qaeda prefers more "bang for their buck" apparently.

You might think its good news that al Qaeda is no longer that interested in a dirty bomb attack. And you'd be dead wrong. The interrogation revealed that al Qaeda is more focused on building something else potentially much more deadly. Something the experts call a crude nuclear bomb. Fortunately for us, developing a conventional nuclear fission bomb is very difficult. The essential ingredients do not exist in nature – they must be manufactured using an expensive, dangerous, and highly sophisticated process. Manufacturing weapons grade nuclear materials is so difficult that even entire countries with large budgets, expert nuclear scientists, and extensive nuclear facilities have great difficulty performing the task. Witness countries like Iran, for example.

A second problem is manufacturing the explosive device itself. Making a fission bomb that is safe, efficient, and small enough to fit inside a bomber or a missile war head is far beyond the means of any terrorist group. Unfortunately for us, terrorists don't care much about safety, efficiency, or size. They just want to blow shit up.

A crude nuclear bomb bypasses most of these issues. It is possible to make a low yield nuclear bomb using a lesser grade of nuclear material – you just need more of it. In order to make a nuclear fission bomb, you must refine naturally occurring uranium. Mined raw uranium contains about 99% of U-238 which is not radioactive enough to create and sustain a nuclear chain reaction. Raw uranium also contains about 0.7% of U-235 which is what you need to make a nuclear explosion. To get enough U-235 to blow something up, you need to refine raw uranium using a very difficult and expensive process known as uranium enrichment. This enrichment process is considered far beyond the means of known terrorist groups. Weapons grade uranium is defined to be at least 90% U-235. Only a few countries have been able to muster the technical sophistication and resources necessary to achieve this. The good news for terrorists and bad news for the rest us is that you can make a nuclear bomb from lesser enriched uranium, even something around 20% pure U-235 might work. The atomic bomb that destroyed Hiroshima used far less pure U-235 than is considered weapons grade by today's standards.

All enriched uranium, whether considered weapons grade or not is highly controlled by most governments. But there are sources available if you have sufficient resources and ingenuity – neither are lacking in organizations like al Qaeda. This is particularly true since the breakup of the old Soviet Union and the rise of the nuclear capabilities in terror sponsoring states like Iran and North Korea. Iran already produces large amounts of enriched uranium, falling just short of the weapons grade designation. But as the world's largest sponsor of anti-Western terrorism, Iran has plenty of enriched uranium suitable for a crude nuclear weapon.

The second problem addressed by a crude nuclear bomb is the explosive mechanism itself. Producing a safe and efficient bomb using the latest in nuclear explosive technology is still beyond the reach of terrorist groups today. But there is a much simpler way – one that was used in the first atomic bomb. It's called a Gun Type Bomb. The concept is easy to understand but somewhat difficult to actually build. Basically, you take two pieces of highly enriched uranium (the less enriched, the more you need) and put them at opposite ends of a gun-like tube. Each piece must be at least two thirds of the critical mass for an explosion. You'd need about sixty kilograms – just over one hundred pounds of the stuff. Uranium is so dense that such an amount would easily fit in a container the size of a one gallon can.

On one end of the tube, you put a conventional propellant (explosive) next to one piece of the uranium. When you detonate the propellant, it drives the uranium at one end of the tube into the piece at the other end achieving the super critical mass necessary for a nuclear explosion. The trick is bringing the two pieces of uranium together fast enough so the reaction does not blow the whole mechanism apart before it can generate an appreciable explosive yield. The basic principles for doing so are widely available in the open literature. To be on the safe side, using more readily available, lower purity enriched uranium, the terrorists would need two to three times the amount required for critical mass.

From beginning to end, the chain reaction achieved in this crude gun-type nuclear bomb lasts only a few millionths of a second. The energy released during this short period would be the equivalent of thousands of tons (kilotons) of TNT. The initial explosion vaporizes the uranium into a gas, quickly ending the chain reaction, but not before it releases a ball of energy with greater temperatures and pressures than found at the center of the sun. Of the original sixty kilograms of uranium used, only about 2% will actually be used up in the nuclear reaction. Not very efficient, but the destructive effects would be immense. The Hiroshima bomb achieved a fifteen-kiloton explosion with a similar bomb. That would be enough to vaporize much of downtown Chicago.

The logistics of building and transporting such a weapon, would be formidable but not insurmountable. The crude gun-type bomb would be heavy, probably about a ton. Such a bomb could easily be carried in a van or a truck. The components of the bomb, the nuclear materials and the explosive device itself, could be delivered separately and assembled at the target location. Surprisingly, enriched uranium is not highly radioactive and can be shielded in small lead containers making it fairly easy to transport without detection. The number of possible pathways to smuggle a nuclear bomb and its ingredients into the United States are immense. The facilities necessary to build or assemble such a crude nuclear bomb need not be sophisticated. South Africa managed to build and assemble its first nuclear bombs in an ordinary looking warehouse. There are at least fifty countries across the world where such bombs could be assembled in areas where the central governments have no reach.

After digesting both the seminar and the classified briefing paper, I was in a state of shock. Somewhere between alarmed and terrified. Being part of the only team standing in the way of a nuclear attack on one's hometown tends to do that to a person.

This is my kind of town, Chicago is
My kind of town, Chicago is
My kind of people, too
People who smile at you.
- My Kind of Town by Sammy Cahn

# 7
# MY KIND OF TOWN

Ever since the terrorism seminar, I've been increasingly frustrated about my inability to help. There's been nothing of note on my future Mega Event radar and I'm feeling useless. By the time something pops up, I'm afraid it may be too late to stop it. Fate can be a bitch like that sometimes.

I vent my frustration during today's phone chat with Special Agent Toomey.

"I'm tired of waiting around for something to happen. There must be something more I can do."

"Like what?"

"Don't you have suspects or UNSUBS or something that you bring in for questioning?"

"We have surveillance on a few suspected members of terror cells, but we don't have enough to bring them in for questioning yet."

"How about you let me talk to them? If they're up to something bad, maybe I'll be able to tell."

"That might be helpful but living in California makes it impractical. We can't just make these people talk to you whenever you happen to be in town."

"What if I was always in town?"

"Are you considering moving back here?"

"No, I love the beach too much. But I could take a leave from work and spend a few weeks up your way."

"We might be able to arrange that. Maybe give you a place to stay and a place to work at the Chicago Field Office. What exactly did you have in mind?"

"I don't know exactly but if you can get me close to some potential suspects, I can take a peek at their immediate futures and maybe see if they're up to something. It only takes a few seconds. I don't even need to talk to them."

"That would be helpful. We could go through a bunch of suspects in just a few hours."

"Find me a place close to downtown that takes dogs and I'm in."

"I'll get right on that. Book your flight with an open return. Not sure how long this will take."

Moments later, I'm making plans for an extended stay in Chicago. I tell my boss I need a temporary leave from the Amazon delivery gig. He says fine but can't guarantee my position will still be there when I return. That's the beauty of having a casual, no pressure job. I don't give a fuck. As for my house, I just close it up and ask Marty to keep an eye on things while I'm gone. He's disappointed to lose his wing man but understands that life throws you curve balls sometimes.

Agent Toomey arranges for a short-term rental on the 25th floor of a high-rise apartment building on Lake Shore Drive and we're all set. As we leave for Chicago, Chewy has a few questions.

"Do they have beaches there?"

"Yes they do, along the lake. Just a short walk from where we'll be staying."

"Will I have a yard?"

"No, but they have a big park close by. We just need to take an elevator down to ground level."

"What's an elevator?"

When we arrive it's early December and already cold as fuck in Chicago. Chewy is a bit shell shocked at all the changes but he's adapting.

"You didn't tell me it'd be so cold. When does it get warm?"

"Not for several months. And even then, it pretty much goes from Artic cold as fuck winter directly to stifling hot as hell summer."

"Every time I pee outside it freezes before it hits the ground. If I had any balls, they'd freeze off too."

"Good thing we took care of that problem, huh?"

"What kind of place is this? I want to go home."

"Toughen up Buttercup. We're here to catch the bad guys remember?"

"Couldn't you have put me into a doggie hotel for a few weeks back at the beach? Or maybe just let me stay home and have one of your beach bitches come by to feed me?"

"You'd miss me too much. Besides, I may need your help sniffing out evil doers."

"My nose is frozen."

"You'll adjust. We'll let your fur grow longer and you'll be fine. Maybe get you some doggie boots so your paws don't freeze to the sidewalk."

"Evil human."

Like I said, he's still adapting.

It's only a short walk from my new apartment on the lake to the FBI field office downtown. But on a cold windy morning, that walk can be life threatening. And today its fifteen degrees below zero without the wind factored in – which is blowing about twenty mph off the lake. You can almost never get a cab or an Uber when the weather is really bad. So, I put on multiple layers of clothing, ski mask, ski parka, gloves, and ski pants before I set out for work. It's been some time since I lived in Chicago, and I make a rookie mistake. I forget about boots – I'm just wearing regular shoes. That mistake becomes clear as I cross the bridge over the rail station from the lake over to downtown. Suddenly, I can no longer feel my toes. Fuck.

I break into a sprint to get across the bridge before frostbite takes both my feet. Once across I can get down into the subway system which connects most of downtown. It's cool, dark, dank, musty, and generally unpleasant in the Chicago underground, but to me if feels like a lifesaving oasis.

No way I'm going back to walk Chewy today. He'll just need to stay inside and use the pee pads. Hey, it's only a rental.

When I finally arrive at the office, Special Agent Toomey is waiting for me.

> Left a good job in the city,
> Workin' for the man ev'ry night and day,
> And I never lost one minute of sleepin',
> Worryin' 'bout the way things might have been.
>   - Proud Mary by Creedence Clearwater Revival

# 8
# WORKING FOR THE MAN

Special Agent Toomey is pleased to see me. I think. It's hard to tell with him. Both corners of his mouth turned up slightly when he saw me. I have a feeling that's as close as he gets to smiling.

"Welcome to the Chicago FBI Field Office Mr. Hedley. A little brisk out there out there this morning I see."

"I can't feel my toes."

"You might want to add some boots to that snow suit you're wearing."

"I forgot how cold the sidewalks can get here. I'll pick up some artic snow boots on my lunch break."

"They sell those in the lobby gift shop. We get a lot of folks from out of town visiting our office."

"When do I get started?"

"We set you up in one of our staff cubicles. Stow your snow gear. Our daily debrief starts in five minutes – main conference room."

Toomey shows me the way to my tiny cubicle. What it lacks in size, it makes up for with technology. A huge computer monitor takes up most of the desk space. It appears to be connected to the FBI main computer – judging by the FBI logo screen saver. I take off several layers of clothing and proceed to the conference room.

The team is already assembled when I arrive. There are about fifteen agents densely packed around an oval table. Most of them look and dress much like Special Agent Toomey. He introduces me to the group, which he calls the "Hot Flash Team". I try not to laugh. These guys really suck at naming things.

Agent Toomey: Mr. Hedley is a private citizen. For the next several weeks, he will be a temporary team member reporting directly to me. His specialty will be HUMINT. Mr. Hedley has cleared a Level 1 Security Screen. We will be seeking additional clearances for him shortly. In the meantime, please confine your briefing statements to Level 1.

I later learned that my HUMINT specialty stands for Human Intelligence. Sounds cool right?

Agent Toomey: SIGINT Go.

SIGINT Guy: We continue to intercept above normal communications traffic from suspicious sources within a twenty-mile radius of Downtown. The volume of such traffic has been steadily increasing over the past twelve weeks. Right now, it stands at 243% of normal. Sources are cloaked and high level encrypted. NSA is tasked with decoding a few of the most suspicious sources, but they'll need several more weeks for a partial decode. Incoming traffic to these sources has been increasing at about the same rate. We still can't pinpoint exact locations, but much of increased traffic comes from the Middle East – particularly Iran. Our most substantial lead so far came last week from the initial NSA encryption decodes. Apparently two words are commonly present in the incoming traffic but are never used in the outgoing, local traffic. Those words are ENRICHED and URANIUM. SIGINT is concerned about what those words might mean in terms of the anticipated Terrorist Action phase.

Agent Toomey: Questions?

No one has any outward reaction to this information, much less a question. Yep, people are planning to vaporize downtown Chicago – just another Tuesday at the FBI Field Office. My personal reaction is more along the lines of "Holy fucking fuck, we're fucked!"

Agent Toomey: HUMINT Go.

HUMINT Guy: Our people on the ground continue to believe that we are dealing with four to five terrorist cells all operating within the same twenty-mile radius of Downtown observed by SIGINT. We have no sources inside these cells as they appear to have completed both Recruitment and Organization / Planning Phases. The cells are likely Islamic extremist in nature, most likely internationally controlled and funded, probably aligned with al Qaeda. We have informants in place watching all commercial points of entry to Chicago including lake, river, air, train, and highway. Commercial cargo inspection sampling has been increased to yield a 75% probability of detection. HUMINT resources have been deployed inside the local supply chains for known arms dealers. So far, we have not detected any significant or unusual activity in these areas. We suspect the terror cells are organized in a typical al Qaeda style ring structure, where each node is only aware of their own particular mission and is only able to contact one or two other nodes. This structure is particularly difficult to infiltrate and roll up since mission plan awareness is highly compartmentalized within each node. Our best shot at infiltrating these cells is to identify and compromise the communications node which has awareness of all other nodes in the ring. We are running surveillance on all known foreign nationals in the area from Middle Eastern countries as well as all their contacts and callers. We have assets on the ground intercepting local burner phone conversations in real time as they are identified by SIGINT. We are running active surveillance on four possible suspects who may be affiliated with these cells. As of now, we have nothing solid on any of them.

Agent Toomey: Questions?

No questions.

Agent Toomey: Surveillance Go.

Surveillance Gal: We have radiation detection assets deployed to all major points of entry to the Chicago area. The detectors have been upgraded to the latest technology and will detect both penetrating gamma radiation as well as mixed alpha, beta, and gamma radiation. In addition, we have 24/7 aerial drone coverage over the entire Chicago Downtown area with both radiation detection and magnetometers. The magnetometers are calibrated to detect any large, dense metallic object over one half ton within one cubic mile. Any crude nuclear detonation device should be detectable if we can get within range. We are less optimistic on the radiation detectors since U-235 is not difficult to shield from detection. Our best bet would be to detect any radiation released from improper handling of these materials during the assembly process. Bank wire transactions for amounts over $10,000 are being monitored for all local banks within 500 miles. All banks in the area are poised to alert us of any cash bank withdrawals over $5,000. We have monitoring in place for any credit / debit card transactions used for explosive materials, guns, and detonation devices. All notary transactions used for Last Will and Testament activity in the Chicago area are being cross referenced with the surveillance list from HUMINT. New warehouse leases over 5,000 square feet are being tracked and all associated lessors and lessees are being turned over to HUMINT. We have not detected any solid leads.

Agent Toomey: Questions? Okay, given the lack of activity we've seen on actual procurement and funding, I think we are still early into Preparatory Conduct phase of this attack – probably still finishing up the planning phase. We are going to move back our estimated timeline for the attack to 100-120 days from now. That puts us in the March – April timeframe. Our nuclear experts believe it would take that long to procure and assemble all the necessary components for a crude nuclear device. That also corresponds roughly to normal al Qaeda timelines once cells enter the Preparatory Conduct phase. We need to continue all ongoing SIGINT, HUMINT, and Surveillance activities at their current levels. Once we get solid leads, I'll request additional resources. I've brought in Mr. Hedley to assist with our HUMINT activities in the paranormal realm. He's had success in the past anticipating people's immediate future activities. The plan is to get Mr. Hedley in sight of a surveillance target. He should be able to tell us if they're up to something suspicious within a few minutes of close proximity. I want each team to give me a list of your highest priority suspects and their normal daily routines. I want updates to that list every day. I'll escort Mr. Hedley on daily reconnaissance missions and make contact with each suspect on your lists. Neither Mr. Hedley nor I will attempt to engage the suspects – we just need to get within sight and confirm their identity. I'll be sending back live video feed to this office in order to confirm identities. We start tomorrow so I'll need your lists by end of day. Questions?

    Not a very chatty group it seems. No questions.
    The winter arctic blast cold wave is still out in force. Agent Toomey took pity on my meager attempts to survive the cold and arranged to pick me up at my apartment for the next few days. Today, we head downtown for a quick encounter with the high priority surveillance targets. Without revealing sources and methods due to my limited security clearance, I learned the basic background of the four suspects.
    All four are young males and are naturalized US citizens with families from the Middle East. They have all been in the country for decades with squeaky clean records – no arrests, no complaints, nothing. They all have steady jobs and generate a lower middle-class income. They speak English well with only slight accents. In short, they dress, act, and look exactly like everyday Americans. The only thing that put them on the FBI radar is their contact with known terror suspects. Apparently, these contacts are frequent and outside of their normal relationships with friends, work relationships, and neighbors. Surveillance of their communications, phones, and computers has not revealed anything out of ordinary. No visits to "Bombs Are Us" or "How to Build a Weapon of Mass Destruction" websites I'm guessing.
    Special Agent Toomey has arranged for us to have a close encounter with two of these suspects today based on their normal weekday habits. One of the two works at Chicago City Hall and typically has lunch in the

first-floor cafeteria whenever the weather is bad – which is certainly the case today. The other is a parking lot attendant at a downtown parking garage and is working at the exit gate today. It should be a simple matter for me to get within just a few feet of both men without raising suspicion.

We start at City Hall for lunch. After a few minutes, Agent Toomey quickly recognizes Suspect #1 and points him out to me. I bow my head so no one can see my crazy eye twitch as I look at this man's immediate future. The headlines I see first are for those people in my immediate presence. Looking further out in my mind, I can see future headlines of other people in my proximity that are further away. Looking out as far as I can see in my mind, I see those headlines merging into Mega Event Streams which contain the headlines of significant future events up to twelve days into the future. Those are the event streams I use to predict hurricanes and now to predict terror attacks. But right now, I am focused on the future headlines of the man sitting at the lunch table next to me.

It doesn't sound like he's having a very eventful day. SUSPECT GETS UP FOR A DRINK REFILL. Not very helpful. Next one: SUSPECT GETS A PHONE CALL FROM MASHA. Okay, that one is worth looking at. Mentally clicking on that headline, I see the details of the call. Masha is one of his good friends and wants to see if he is free for a drink after work. Nothing nefarious about that. The remainder of his headlines were equally innocuous. I tell Agent Toomey about the phone call and sure enough, after a few minutes, our suspect gets a phone call. The HUMINT team will likely surveil that Happy Hour meet up, but Agent Toomey doesn't believe anything will come of it. Apparently, they know all about Masha and don't consider him to be anyone of interest.

Next, we visit the parking garage where the second suspect is working. We park for a while in Toomey's unmarked car to avoid a suspicious immediate exit. As we pull up to the lot exit gate, Toomey points out the man in the booth confirming he is our suspect. I turn the other way as I look at this man's future headlines. The first few headlines are routine events for a parking lot attendant – nothing worth enhanced surveillance. Towards the end of his twelve-minute stream of future headlines, I notice this: SUSPECT REMINDS BOSS HE NEEDS TO LEAVE WORK EARLY TODAY. I look closer at that one for details. Our suspect has already told his boss that he needs to leave early today and just wants to remind him. I can tell from the headline description that this meeting is important to him, and he seems rather concerned about it. There are no details about the meeting, but our suspect arranges to leave work at four PM.

We depart the parking garage and I tell Agent Toomey about this meeting. This is a new development. There have been no prior intercepted communications about such a meeting. Suspect #2 does not have a burner phone and is subject to almost constant HUMINT surveillance so it's unlikely he could have set up such an encounter through any normal means. Toomey tells me the most likely way such a meeting could be arranged is through something called a "Dead Drop". That's spy talk for leaving a message at an agreed location for another person to pick up later. An agent, or terrorist in this case, uses an agreed signal to alert the other person that a dead drop is going to occur. That signal is usually something inconspicuous like pulling down a shade or making a chalk mark somewhere. Once the signal is observed, the message recipient goes to the agreed location and picks up the message. These locations can be any public place, under a park bench, under a rock, in a public toilet – anywhere easily accessible but not easily seen by a passerby. Often the sender and receiver of the message are unknown to each other and have never met. Al Qaeda terror cells often use third party "Cut Outs" to pick up and deliver these messages. The Cut Outs typically don't know either party by name. All this spy craft makes the terrorist cells difficult to discover and roll up. Unless you have me on your side.

Agent Toomey notifies HUMINT to double the surveillance on Suspect #2 so they can follow him to his meeting, wherever that might be. Toomey wants to risk another encounter with Suspect #2 just before he leaves to see if I can pick up the meeting time and location. I smile and tell him that should not be necessary. You see once I tap into a person's Event Stream of future headlines, I can usually locate that person's Event Stream later even if they are not in my immediate proximity. It's almost like GPS tracking. Event Streams have a kind of personal identifier – an ID code of sorts. All I need to do is look at all the Event Streams around me and locate that particular one. I don't know exactly how far away I can be from a person to see their future, but I know it extends out at least a few miles. Bottom line is I can be in the café across the street from the parking garage and still pick out Suspect #2's Event Stream. And I can keep checking it every twelve minutes until I find out something about the meeting. Agent Toomey is impressed.

It doesn't take long. About thirty minutes after Suspect #2 leaves work, I look at his Event Stream and see this headline: SUSPECT MEETS WITH JERRY. Turns out Suspect #2 has gone home to shower and change. He plans to slip out the back door, hail a cab, and go meet Jerry. I've no idea who Jerry might be (not exactly a name that screams Islamic Terrorist) but I do know where this meeting will be and exactly what time it will take place. I also know that Suspect #2 is the one who asked for the meeting and is very anxious about it.

All of this gives Agent Toomey time to set up surveillance at the meeting site. He arranges for the location – a small dive on the North Side called the Crowbar – to be bugged at all the tables and the bar. Agents will be inside the bar as well. A van outside will use long range video cameras to record the whole thing and coordinate all surveillance activity. I'll be in the van as well to warn the HUMINT team of any unforeseen developments that may occur.

Everything is in place when Suspect #2 walks into the bar. There's only a handful of people hanging out at the Crowbar and two of them are FBI. No one, including Suspect #2 seems to know which one is Jerry. He reveals himself by raising his arm in welcome. They're seated at a secluded spot in the far corner of the bar. The hastily set up mike has a bad connection. We can barely make out a few words, but the video is excellent. One thing is clear – the conversation is intense and there's tension in the air. We only hear about every third word, but it becomes clear that Suspect #2 wants out of whatever deal Jerry is offering. Agent Toomey shoots me a worried looks and I quickly check Jerry's Event Stream. I scan the headlines for the next twelve minutes of Jerry's life. It turns out he doesn't have that long. JERRY ORDERS A BUD LIGHT. Okay, he's got crap taste in beer, but that doesn't make him a criminal. JERRY SAYS HIS PRAYERS. Maybe it's that time of day for Muslims? JERRY BLOWS UP THE CROWBAR. That's going to happen in two minutes and there are no alternative outcomes available in the Event Stream.

"Tell your agents to get the fuck out of the bar NOW! Jerry's got a bomb!"

Toomey immediately radios instructions for his agents to leave. They don't hesitate. As they approach the door, both yell out "Everybody get out! There's a bomb!" A few savvy Chicagoans heed their warning and follow them out the door. Ten seconds later an explosion blows out every window on the block and rocks our surveillance van. The next day, the Chicago Tribune and Sun Times will report that a gas line explosion rocked the North Side. Four people were killed instantly including Jerry, Suspect #2, and two other unlucky bar patrons. The FBI agents escaped with only minor injuries.

Surveillance video was used to identify Jerry within an hour of the blast. Turns out he is a known mid-level al Qaeda operative – never before seen in Chicago. That alone tells us something big is happening. Agent Toomey can't tell me much, but within hours the Terrorism Threat Level is raised from Yellow to Orange for the entire Chicago area.

And I be taking care of business (every day),
Taking care of business (every way),
I've been taking care of business (it's all mine),
Taking care of business and working overtime.
- Taking Care of Business by Bachman-Turner Overdrive

# 9
# TAKING CARE OF BUSINESS

Ever since I saved our two HUMINT agents from almost certain incineration, the Hot Flash Team has shown me newfound respect. Not that anyone besides me would ever be able tell – their FBI, Joe Friday demeanors are darn near inscrutable. Now when I speak during the daily briefings, every eye in the room is on me with rapt attention. I wonder if these people ever even blink, such is their intensity. But now occasionally, in hallways or during lunch, a few of these agents will pat my shoulder as we pass or grunt something that sounds like "How's it goin'?" Ms. Surveillance (her actual name is Agent Fields, but I recently learned her first name is Rebecca) has actually chatted me up a bit in the hallway. If it weren't for that Sig pistol on her hip, I could swear she might be flirting with me. Anyway, she's pretty attractive in a hot, pistol carrying law enforcement kind of way. A far cry from my usual Beach Babes that's for sure.

Special Agent Toomey and I have been doing daily encounters with every Hot Flash Team suspect, including Suspect #3 and #4 on the terror cell list. So far, all I've uncovered is a very boring list of everyday events. We must keep repeating these encounters in hopes that one of the suspects will be up to something within the next twelve minutes. It's tedious, unfulfilling work – that is until someone decides to blow something up in the next few minutes.

It suddenly occurs to me that we are not using the full potential of my capabilities in this effort. Well not exactly my capabilities.

"Hey Toomey. I just thought of something. You remember my dog, Chewy?"

"Yeah, your dog that talks to you. So?"

"He might be able to help us."

"How the hell can a Golden Doodle help with a terrorism investigation?"

"Chewy has this ability – well all dogs have it really, but he is the only one that can tell anyone about it. Chewy is able to tell good people from bad people just by the way they smell."

"And that would help us how?"

"Well one thing that's been frustrating our investigation is that I can only tell so much about a person by looking at the next twelve minutes of their lives. I mean most people, even the bad ones, lead pretty mundane lives most of the time. The chances that I'll discover anything important about them in just that short time slice are pretty low. I can't really tell what kind of person they are or if they merit further investigation – unless they happen to be involved in something nefarious within the next twelve minutes. Chewy on the other hand, should be able to tell us – well me to be precise – whether a suspect is a person of good intention or not."

"Wait a minute. Didn't you tell me that Chewy said I smelled bad when we first met?"

"Tell me Special Agent Toomey, when you first came to see me, did you have good intentions? I seem to recall you saying something about putting me and my best friend in a Federal penitentiary for twenty years. Minimum."

"That was for the greater good – at least in my mind."

"Chewy's frame of reference for "good" is whether it's good for me – well actually whether it's good for him. He's a bit self-centered that way. Luckily, what's good for him is also usually good for me. Putting me in jail was certainly not good for me or him. So, to Chewy, you smelled bad."

"So how do we know whether Chewy will sense a terrorist has good intentions or not?"

"Chewy is smarter than you think. But you don't need to be a doggie rocket scientist to know that anyone planning to vaporize the town where you eat, sleep, and poop doesn't have the best intentions. That person is going to smell really bad to Chewy."

"I guess that would help focus our efforts on the bad guys. Maybe even eliminate some suspects if Chewy turns out to be as accurate as you say. How would you go about this?"

"I'm thinking we get Chewy a Service Dog certificate. They're ridiculously easy to get these days and Chewy could certainly pass any test required. That way we could take him into any public place where we might encounter a suspect."

"That might actually work. Are you sure Chewy will do it?"

"It won't be easy to convince him, but I think so. Chewy hates the cold weather, though."

"Come on, it's already warming up here a little."

"Yeah, it's gone all the way from *I'm Pretty Sure I'm Going to Die Cold* to *Goddamn I Can't Feel My Toes Cold*."

"You wimps from SoCal can't appreciate the change of seasons."

I refrained from pointing out that Chicago only has two seasons – Hot as Fuck and Cold as Fuck. That evening, I discuss my idea with Chewy.

"So, your plan is for me to spend my days in the frozen streets of Chicago trying to smell random people looking for bad guys?"

"I'd be right there with you pointing out the people of interest."

"Except you'll be wearing warm boots and a North Face parka. I just have my short hair and bare paws. Plus, my hair hasn't grown out yet from that ridiculous poodle cut you gave me."

"Yeah, that was unfortunate. I didn't mean for the groomer to poodle my doodle quite so much. How about we get you a doggie jacket and boots?"

"That's so lame. No way am I wearing cutesy doggie clothes."

"How about we get you something in leather? You'll look like a biker dog. Complete with biker boots."

"You can do that?"

"Hey, I'm a Level 1 HUMINT Security Consultant for the crack FBI Hot Flash Team. I'm sure I can get them to round up some special surveillance gear for you."

"Sounds impressive. How about some night vision goggles?"

"Won't go with the outfit."

"I want a title like you. Maybe head of the DOGINT team. Special Agent Chewy - DOGINT. You can call me SAC-D for short. That has a nice ring to it."

"I'll look into it."

"Tell Agent PISSANT to make it happen."

It took some explaining, but Agent Toomey finally agreed to Chewy's demands. Sort of. He got the leather dog jacket and boots along with a service dog certificate with an honorary title and an FBI logo. Chewy can't read but he's impressed with the FBI logo. I've asked the team to call him SAC-D just so he feels important.

Now let me tell you something, Streebeck.
There are two things that clearly differentiate the human species from animals.
One, we use cutlery. Two, we're capable of controlling our sexual urges.
Now, you might be an exception, but don't drag me down into your private Hell.
- Detective Joe Friday, Dragnet

# 10
# SPECIAL AGENT CHEWY

Chewy is letting this special agent thing go to his fuzzy head. Don't get me wrong, he's a huge asset to our investigation, but he's become very demanding. Now even I have to call him SAC-D. And it's not just Agent Chewy. It's got to be *Special* Agent Chewy. When he pisses me off (regularly), I've taken to calling him NO SAC. Turns out Chewy is good at puns, and he becomes instantly enraged. Which of course encouraged me call him that regularly. Not in front of our FBI colleagues, though – I know where to draw the line. SAC or NO SAC, he has teeth after all.

Aside from the Prima Donna issue, Chewy and I have settled nicely into our new surveillance roles. Agent Toomey gives us our assignments each morning. He gives us photographs, times, and map locations where the suspects of the day are expected. Chewy and I head out with his service dog biker outfit and look for the suspects. It's hard to maintain a low profile. Chewy attracts a good deal of attention. Between his leather doggie jacket, complete with studded collar, and his biker boots with prominent steel buckles, he resembles something you might see at a pet friendly gay biker bar. I just tell him he looks cool.

Here's what our typical surveillance mission is like. Chewy and I look at the suspect's photograph. Today we are assigned Suspect 39, aka Herbie Smite. Apparently, you can't identify potential terror suspects just by their names. We are not given any other information about Herbie lest it color SAC-D's Good Guy vs. Bad Guy verdict. Chewy would prefer an item of the suspect's clothing as an identifier but we don't have that. We go to the appointed place and time where the suspect is supposed to be. Typically, it's a lunch spot, a park, or a residential street. Today it's a take-out hot dog joint. Herbie likes Chicago Style hotdogs it seems. He's not there, so Chewy and I cool our heals walking around the general vicinity. It's freezing outside but at least now we both have warm clothes so our heals are only cool, not frostbit. After several minutes, Herbie finally shows up and orders his lunch. Chewy and I casually (as casual as you can be walking a dog dressed up like a singer from the Village People) walk over to Herbie and give him a good sniff. Sometimes it takes Chewy several sniffs to get a firm impression. The first time we encountered a Bad Guy, our crack DOGINT agent decided to let me know by peeing on the suspect's leg. It took a few trial runs to break him of that habit. Now he just tells me directly once we are safely out of pee range.

Chewy: Herbie's OK. He's no saint but he's probably not going to blow up Chicago.

Me: No shit Sherlock. The guy is named after a cartoon car. Not exactly my idea of a prime terror suspect.

Chewy: Like you would know. I'm pretty sure he beats up his girlfriend though.

Me: You can tell that from his smell?

Chewy: I can tell he had sex this morning and he still had some female blood on his fingers. Not exactly a boy scout.

Me: Way to go SAC-D! Very impressive.

Chewy: Any dog could have told you that – if they could talk to you. I can also tell you what he had for breakfast.

Me: Damn.

Chewy and I return to the office and make our report. I type it up on my FBI computer while SAC-D chews on my shoelaces. I leave out the part about Herbie's violent sex life.
As we head back out for our next case, I run into Agent Fields in the hallway. She looks ready for action with that sexy Sig pistol on her hip and handcuffs attached to her belt just above her fine-looking ass.
"Going out to catch some bad guys, Agent Fields? It looks like you're ready to do some damage."
"Just some routine surveillance, Hedley. Of course, if anyone tries to mess with me, they're going to be sorry. How about you and SAC-D there?"
Chewy looks pleased she's referred to him by his official name.
"Just heading out to vet another suspect with my furry bad guy detector."
That makes her smile – an expression that completely transforms her appearance from bad ass FBI agent to fun, attractive woman. I wasn't expecting that.

"You should smile more often Agent Fields. It becomes you. Call me Jake if you like."

A brief flicker of indecision appears on her face which is quickly followed by a flirtatious grin. This is rather unexpected. We definitely need to see where this goes.

"Agent Fields: OK Jake but only if you call me Beck. It's short for Rebecca."

I've been around the FBI office for a few weeks now, and never have I heard anyone call her Beck. This is getting interesting. Chewy is making impatient doggie noises which I ignore. We've got a few minutes to spare before our next suspect typically takes his walk in the park.

"You know Beck, Chewy and I haven't seen much of Chicago yet. Do you know the city well?"

"Lived here all my life. I can show you around if you like. Keep you out of trouble maybe."

"That's a lot to ask, especially the trouble part. What do you have in mind?"

"How about I show you the Art Institute on Saturday? They're having a special Picasso exposition. We can have lunch after if you like."

"Okay, I'm in. Chewy is fine on his own for a few hours."

Chewy: What now?

"It's a date then. I'll call you on Saturday morning to finalize. See you around Jake."

And off she goes. I can't help but watch her handcuffs sashay in time with her hips as she walks off.

"Did you see what happened there? I think she just asked me out on a date."

"Good for you. I'm going to be stuck in the apartment on Saturday while you walk around with Agent Hot Ass pretending to be looking at the paintings."

"Not necessarily. I really do like Picasso."

"I don't know anything about art, but unless Picasso paints strippers in 3D, you'll have your eyes on Beck's ass the whole time."

"Picasso does paint nudes a lot, but typically in the Analytic Cubism style. His strippers all have their body parts in the wrong locations."

"So, no competition for Agent Field's ass then?"

"Not even a little. Don't wait up."

Chewy and I head out to meet our next suspect. Another not so bad, bad guy. Truth is I'm still a bit distracted by Agent Fields' rather aggressive dating approach. My suspect report is a bit short on details.

Friday afternoon finally rolls around and I'm more nervous than usual for a first date. I've never dated law enforcement before. Hell, I don't date at all really. I wonder what the first date protocol would be for an FBI agent packing heat. I decide to just play it by ear. That usually turns out okay. I'm tempted to peek into my future but this time I think I'd rather be surprised.

That is until some of my male FBI colleagues brief me on Agent Fields' dating habits. Turns out she's a bit kinky. Not like I have any room to talk on that score, but I'm intrigued. I probe for a few details.

Me: Kinky how?

Male Agent 1: Word is she likes to wind up her dates by handcuffing them to her bed and interrogating them.

Me: No way!

Male Agent 2: That's the word on the street. I hear that her interrogation techniques can be a bit rough.

Me: Thanks for letting me know. I'll be careful.

Male Agent 1: It won't help.

Now I really am nervous. But also, more excited to see what happens. I formulate a plan to deal with my kinky FBI dom date.

Hurt so good,
Come on baby, make it hurt so good.
Sometimes love don't feel like it should,
You make it hurt so good
 -Hurts So Good by John Cougar Mellencamp

# 11
# HURTS SO GOOD

Agent Fields calls me as promised to confirm our date. We arrange to meet at the Art Institute. So far, everything sounds relaxed and normal. Just two people getting together to enjoy some modern art. No hint of sexual undertones or handcuffs. Maybe those crazy FBI agents were just pulling my chain.

There she is right on time waiting by the front entrance. Agent Fields, whom I've now promised to call Beck, is looking good. She's still wearing tight slacks but is now sporting a ruffled V-neck top under her jacket. She looks softer and more feminine than usual with her breasts now competing for attention with her ass.

"Are you ready to see some Cubism, Beck?"

"Always. Picasso has a way of cutting to the chase with his painting. Makes me horny."

"Lucky me."

"We'll see."

Normally, an exchange like that would set my motor running. Now it just makes me anxious for what she may have in store for me later. Being a cool-ass FBI HUMINT consultant, I take it all in stride and proceed with our date.

We linger on several of Picasso's female portraits. Beck seems fascinated.

"This one intrigues me. She portrays both an idealized standard of womanhood and blatant sexuality."

"Her boobs are in the wrong places."

"Women can be full of surprises."

Gulp. Suddenly my cool-ass FBI demeanor is waning. Nevertheless, I press on.

"I love surprises."

"Now that's surprising coming from someone who regularly sees the future in advance."

"That's why I don't peek ahead unless it's for the general good."

"Good. We should get along fine then. Got to let a girl have her mystery."

After thoroughly checking out the Picasso exhibit, we tour the Institute's wide collection of Impressionist paintings. Beck has seen them many times, but for me it's been years. Getting lost in the beauty of the art, I almost forget what may lay in store for me later. Almost.

After a quick lunch, Beck offers to show me a bit of downtown which Chicagoans affectionately call "The Loop". I've seen it many times, but not with a sexy tour guide, so off we go. Not surprisingly, we pass by her apartment, and she invites me in for a drink. I sense a trap is about to be sprung, so of course I am cautious.

"Are you planning to seduce me, Agent Fields? Whatever, I'm in."

"You did say you liked surprises and I do make a decent martini. Let's just see how it goes."

I retreat to the restroom while Beck fixes the drinks. Her apartment is sparsely decorated, neat and efficient. Much like the lady herself. The bedroom door is closed, but in my imagination, it is adorned with silk sheets and red leather.

In the interest of self-preservation, I take a quick peek at the next twelve minutes. Nothing out of the ordinary.

Beck does make a pretty good martini. Kettle One. Shaken. Blue cheese olives. She begins to smile more as the martini's flow. I ask her what she likes about working for the FBI. She says the usual stuff about protecting the world from bad guys. I sense it's more than that.

"Nothing to do with those sexy handcuffs you wear all the time?"

"You noticed."

"Couldn't help it. They are stationed right above that sexy ass of yours."

"Do you know where I keep my pistol?"

"Hip holster and another in your ankle holster. But not today."

"Pretty observant of you Mr. Hedley. What else have you noticed?"

"You have amazing gray eyes. I imagine people have a hard time lying to you."

"Sometimes they try but I usually get to the truth eventually."

"How do you do that?"

"I could show you if you want."

I turn away from her and look out the window. Seems like a good time to take another look at the next twelve minutes. Twitch, twitch and a bold headline appears in my head: **SEXY FBI AGENT HANDCUFFS JAKE TO HER BED**. I take a closer look at the details. Beck has stripped off her clothes and is wearing a black corset, heels, and stockings. Nothing else. I am tied spread eagle on her bed. She has a riding crop in her hand. Quickly I look for an alternative outcome that better aligns with my sexual proclivities. Here's one: **JAKE SURPRISES SEXY FBI AGENT AND HANDCUFFS HER TO THE BED**. It's got a flashing red light above it that tells me I can select that outcome and change the future. Now admittedly, I did take a second to think about it – I mean she did go to all this trouble. Maybe it would be fun. Nope. I press the fuck out of that button.

Next thing I know, Beck's hands are handcuffed to her bed posts and she's looking up at me in shock. She does have that black corset thing on though.

"What the fuck Hedley?"

"I liked your idea - I just flipped the script a bit. Turns out we have similar interests, but I like being the one in charge. Relax Agent Fields, I'm pretty good at this."

"When I get out of this, you are going to be one sorry FBI Consultant."

"Seems like if you had your way, I'd be even sorrier. Let's try it my way and see what happens."

I look over the box of toys she had ready for me. This goes way beyond my fuzzy red handcuffs. I don't even know what half these things are for. But I don't ask her. It would destroy the mood. I just start trying stuff.

Beck: You know that's not where that goes right?

Me: I like to be creative. To go my own way with things.

Beck: Next time I'll label everything for you.

I take my time and pretend she's my suspect with something to hide. Eventually I make her tell me her secrets – at least the sexual ones. We explore all her toys. The whole Fifty Shades of Grey prop department. After a bit of feigned outrage, she eventually settled into her role of suspect. Soon she was confessing things left and right. I went down my preplanned list of questions: Have you ever had sex with a woman? Duh. What's the kinkiest thing you've ever done? Have you ever dreamed of being of being overpowered by a sexy man? Woman? What do you think about when you touch yourself? What makes you cum the hardest? What toys do you like the best? I was very thorough.

It turns out that Beck is multi-orgasmic. In Beck's case, "multi" turned out to be about ten times. Once you get her going, she's not very picky about what goes where. Made for a fun interrogation.

"Please, I can't take anymore! I've told you everything."

"Finally. My hand was getting tired."
"How did you know I would like this?"
"Sexy woman wearing handcuffs all day? Educated guess."
"What are you going to do now?"
"I could just let you up and then let myself out. But I'd rather stay and see how much fun we can have without all the toys. You choose."
"I don't think I can cum anymore, but I'd like to try that second one."
"Tied or untied?"
"Might was well go with what's working."

Gotta love a girl who knows what she wants.

Drop dead legs, pretty smile
Hurts my head, gets me wild
- Drop Dead Legs by Van Halen

# 12
# DEAD DROP

It's now mid-March in Chicago. The weather still mostly sucks but now it has wild variations from artic cold blasts to winter blizzard conditions to unseasonably warm days. All of which can happen in the same week. Today's highs are in the low sixties under sunny skies. Later this week a foot of snow is forecasted. Keeping an eye on the weather in Chicago is a matter of survival. No need for those sexy TV weather girls in tight mini dresses like we have in LA. They are necessary for viewership in SoCal since we really don't have any weather there. The weather reports here are always popular even without any sexual enhancements.

The Hot Flash Team has moved well beyond the original four suspects. Technically, beyond the original three suspects since one is now burned to a crisp. Chewy and I have been able to expand the suspect count to twelve really bad, bad guys all of which are now under intense FBI surveillance. None of the twelve are directly involved in core operations so they don't know anything about the ultimate terrorist act being planned. All are involved in various support actions. Agent Toomey thinks we are still three to five cell members away from the critical Operations Ring. Once we uncover that cell, we should be able to roll up the whole operation – or at least uncover their plans and stop them. We probably only have another month to do so before Chicago is dust.

Chewy and I have been working non-stop trying to find the critical missing links in the terrorist rings. We are making good progress – mostly eliminating potential suspects but occasionally finding new ones. It doesn't leave me a lot of time to explore my new hobby of seeking new ways to extract information from Beck. I have learned quite a bit though.

Beck has always been dominate in her relationships with both men and women. Those relationships are typically short and intense. She really doesn't have time for much else. That explains why she was so efficient in starting up with me I guess – no time for being coy.

I did manage to teach Beck a few things – at least she says I did. The big thing was to help her accept that she does have a submissive side and that it can be a big stress relief to give up control occasionally. She didn't want to embrace that side of herself, but she says it's definitely growing on her. I notice she's more relaxed at work these days – not so stiff. She smiles more often, especially at me.

I doubt Beck and I will last beyond this assignment, but for now it's a great distraction from the stress of trying to save Chicago. After that, I'm guessing Beck will return to her normal dating habits.

Right now, I'm taking Chewy for a walk in the park. Taking advantage of this rare warm and sunny winter day in Chicago. I haven't had any messages from Jennifer in quite some time, but Chewy and I still look for her most every day. Just in case. Today there are several women strolling through the park. Some are even wearing shorts and tank tops taking advantage of the chance to ditch their winter clothes for a day. Most of them eventually walk up to Chewy and make a big fuss over him. He loves that and I enjoy the attention too. None of them are Jennifer. Chewy would let me know.

Eventually, we make our way back to the office. Agent Toomey has a high priority suspect he wants us to check out. Suspect 84 has been under surveillance for about a week from both SIGINT and HUMINT. He picked up a dead drop note from one of SAC-D's bad guys. The note was coded but we have a partial decode. Something about a special package arriving soon. I'll have Chewy check him out, but chances are he's one of the bad ones. I'll take a quick peek into his future to see what I can find out as well. Once I tune into his "wavelength", I won't even have to be close to him next time I want to see his future.

Other HUMINT agents will be in the field with us, just in case. This guy could be dangerous. He's a UPS driver so we know where he should be. The FBI can track any delivery truck equipped with GPS which of course is all of them. They also know the delivery schedules and locations. All we have to do is wait for him to show up at one of his appointed delivery locations. In this case, it's a charming brownstone apartment on the West Side. Chewy and I position ourselves to enter the front door of the brownstone just as the UPS truck drives up. Suspect 84 is a white male with no facial hair. He looks pretty much like your typical UPS delivery guy. Chewy goes into SAC-D mode and gives him a good sniff as we pass by. I look away and gaze into his immediate future. He's got ten more deliveries to do and none of them involve bomb parts. Chewy's assessment is more revealing.

Chewy: This guy is really bad. The worst smell ever. He must be like a serial killer or something.

Me: Can you smell anything more specific?

Chewy: I'm pretty sure he's killed someone in the last twenty-four hours or so. There's fresh blood on his scent. Lots of it.

Me: I'll call Toomey right away to let him know. We'll file the report later.

The Hot Flash Team is monitoring Suspect 84's burner phone in real time now. If he tries to use another one, they'll immediately grab the signal from that one as well. It's just a matter of time before he contacts another cell member or leads us to a critical piece of the terrorist plan. He's our best lead so far. Toomey has me in an FBI surveillance van tailing his every move. They hope to keep me in range to check his future every 30 minutes or so. Chewy gets to ride along as well in case we encounter any other sniff-worthy suspects for SAC-D.

Eventually, I learn that Suspect 84's real name is Dan Jacobs. Toomey doesn't want me to know any details around Jacob's identify for fear it might color my assessment. Plus, I still have a limited security clearance. After two boring days of tailing him in multiple surveillance vans, we finally catch a break. Jacobs' home has been wired for both audio and video. We catch him encoding a note for a Dead Drop. We can't read the encoding, but it's a simple matter for me to check his immediate future which makes his intentions clear. Jacobs is writing a note to the Materials Acquisition cell leader. He doesn't know what is being acquired or why, but he is passing along information on cost and delivery times. The note will be picked up by a third party Cut Out whose identity is unknown to Jacobs. But now we know the location of the drop, so we can follow the thread back to the other cell leader. Hopefully.

Now our surveillance focus shifts to the Dead Drop location. We don't know the exact time of the pickup – not even Jacobs knows that – so we run surveillance round the clock. I am constantly on call to respond whenever the Cut Out arrives. It takes another day and a half, but finally the Cut Out arrives. She looks like a college student trying to earn a few extra bucks. And that's exactly what Toomey believes she may be. I check her future as she approaches the drop – the coded note is taped to the underside of an old pier on Lake Michigan near Rogers Park Beach. Her name is Gwen, and she is studying Communications at Northwestern. An apt major considering her current job choice. Gwen wades through the cold, shallow water and collects the note from under the pier. She's planning to go shopping later for a sexy but not too revealing dress for this weekend's outing with the girls - right after she drops off this note to an address of a person she's never met. I relay that address to the team and within a minute they have the names, photos, and background of everyone who lives at that address. It's a converted warehouse loft apartment building on the North Side. Fairly swanky but not conspicuous. Toomey says there is a good chance the ringleader does not even live there – it probably belongs to someone away on vacation. Sure enough, it turns out the tenant is one, Sam Galinsky and he is currently visiting his parents in Tampa. Gwen is planning to slip the note under the door and get on her way to her shopping expedition. She's already been paid by a fellow student who told her all this was for a rich person treasure hunt. It was enough to pay for her party dress this weekend.

We watch in the van as Gwen slips the note under the door without ringing the bell. No one comes to door, so we wait. Fourteen hours later at about 2:15 AM, a man in dark clothing arrives and opens the door. After just a few minutes, he leaves the apartment with the note. We've installed a night vision camera in the entry way so we can clearly see him slip the note into his right jacket pocket. We could pick him up for questioning, but Toomey thinks we may learn more just by following his activities. As he walks out of the apartment, I take a peek at his next 12 minutes.

Jackpot. The guy's name is Kevin Healy. I see that he's about to read that note once he arrives back at his flat ten minutes from now. The note gives Kevin the details he needs to acquire an electronic fuse mechanism from a local purveyor of illegal arms. Kevin doesn't know or care what the fuse may be for, but given its sophistication and size, he believes it must be for a large bomb. Kevin hopes so. He likes to see things blow up. I pass along the name of the arms dealer and the specs for the fuse to the Hot Flash Team.

Toomey believes that Kevin Healy is not the Acquisition Team leader because he is not privy to all the details of the materials being acquired. That much is clear from my short glimpse into his future. Which means that Healy probably doesn't even know the identity of the team leader. Our best hope is that Healy will contact the Communications Lead of his ring in order to pass along an update to the Team Lead. Once we track down the Communication Lead, we'll be able to uncover all the other members of the Acquisition Team Cell and, just maybe, gain access to the Operations Cell where all the key leadership of this terrorist operation reside.

That's the good news. That bad news is that this fuse is not designed for a chemical bomb. It's a nuclear fuse, one intended to survive a few milliseconds after the initial detonation in order to achieve maximum effect.

April gave us springtime
And the promise of the flowers
And the feeling that we both shared
And the love that we called ours
 - Pieces of April by Dave Loggins

# 13
# APRIL IN CHICAGO

Even during the greatest terror threat in history, Chewy and I still manage to find time for a walk in the park. It's April now and the weather is starting to improve. Now it rains most days. The kind of rain that whips off the lake and cuts right through you. If April showers bring May flowers in Chicago, those must be some strong-ass flowers. Other days it snows.

Today we are lucky. It's rather warm and the sun is shining. There are lots of people walking their dogs in the park. Chewy is happily sniffing the new grass sprouts just beginning to pop out of the frozen ground. As usual, he attracts a crowd of mostly young women, all anxious to meet my dog. These days, Chewy resembles a big furry teddy bear. A badass biker teddy bear. Irresistible to women of all ages, but particularly those under thirty.

As we approach a group of such twenty somethings, Chewy strikes a pose and prepares for extreme attention. Sometimes I wish I were hairy and cute.

Strolling Girl #1: OH MY GOD! What kind of dog is that?
Strolling Girl #2: He looks just like a big teddy bear!
Strolling Girl #3: Can we hug him and pet him?
Me: He's a Golden Doodle and yes, you can pet him. His name is Chewy.

I'm thinking I should be charging admission for this. Maybe negotiate some petting for Chewy's owner at least. As my imagination runs wild with that thought, I shift my gaze to the far end of the park. There walks another lovely young lady who appears to be looking my way. Even at this distance, I can tell she is striking and a bit older than the current group fondling my dog. Maybe she'll come over if I can shake Chewy loose from his pack of adoring fans.

Me: Come on Chewy, let's get you some exercise.

Chewy: Say what now?

With that, I pull firmly on his lead and direct him away from his groupies. We head over in the general direction of that lovely young lady. From here I can tell she has long, brown hair and a cute little wiggle to her walk. She's wearing jeans with a fuzzy sweater top – very appropriate for a sunny April day in Chicago. As she approaches, I can see that her jeans are tight, and her legs are long. Come on Chewy, work your magic!

Sure enough, she heads right over, ignores me, and starts petting Chewy while babbling puppy talk.

Leggy Brown-Haired Girl: Such a Good Boy! YES HE IS. YESSS HE ISSSSS!!!

Me: So how about me? Am I a good boy too?

Leggy Brown-Haired Girl: Probably not, but you must be okay if your dog likes you.

Me: His name is Chewy. He's a Golden Doodle.

Chewy is enthralled. His tail is actually vibrating. Nice to see him having fun. It has been a while since the weather allowed for a walk in the park.

Leggy Brown-Haired Girl: I'm April. Cute dog you have there. What's a Golden Doodle?

Me: He's a cross between a Golden Retriever and a Poodle. Hyper allergenic and no shedding.

April: So, is this how you pick up girls? Using your Doodle as bait?

I'm just about to say "Seems to be working so far" when I stop dead in my tracks and look down at Chewy. His eyes are sparkling.

Chewy: She's the one Jake. She's Jennifer. Her scent is unforgettable.

I'm frozen with shock. I sensed there was something familiar about this girl but not this. She doesn't look at all like Jennifer. She's not blonde. She's clearly not Cuban. She looks to be Scandinavian or Northern European. Tall and dark and lovely. I recall what Jennifer said in her note to me when she left. That Chewy would someday guide me back to her. And then I remember what Chewy told me. That she won't look the same.

That she'll have another name and another background. But he'll recognize her scent. Her beautiful, off the charts smell of pure goodness. He'll know her right away.

"Cat got your tongue, Doodle Boy?"
"Sorry, you just reminded me of someone I used to know."
"And there's the pickup line. Classic."
"Actually, you've thrown me off my game a bit April. My name is Jake. Jake Hedley. My dog really likes you."
"He does seem familiar. I like him too. You seem a bit weird though."
"I tend to grow on people after a while."
"Like warts?"
"Let me start again. Pleased to meet you, April. Want to grab some coffee with Chewy and me?"
"Well, I do like coffee. Not that cheap crap from the food truck. I want a vanilla latte. Extra hot."
"Just like you."
"That's better. Maybe there's hope for you yet."
"Great. There's a Starbucks down the street."

And with that, the three of us head off for some non-crappy coffee. Just me, Chewy, and the long-lost love of my life who looks totally different and doesn't know me. Should make for a fun conversation.

Half-birds, half beautiful maidens, the Sirens were singing enchantresses capable of luring passing sailors to their islands, and, subsequently, to their doom. Daughters of the river god Achelous and a Muse, they were fated to die if anyone should survive their singing. When Odysseus passed them by unharmed, they hurled themselves into the sea and were drowned.

- 12th Book of Homers Odyssey and the origin of the Starbucks Coffee logo

# 14
# THE SIREN'S SONG

April and I wait in line to order our coffee with Chewy in tow. I can't wait to see how she orders. Over the years, I've developed this test to evaluate whether someone is high maintenance. If someone, particularly a woman, orders their coffee with more than two unnecessary modifiers, they are, ipso facto, HIGH MAINTENANCE and are best avoided. Jennifer liked her lattes strong, so she ordered a double shot. One extra modifier. Perfectly acceptable and reasonable for someone who needs an extra jolt of caffeine. Not like some people that order theirs Extra Hot. What does extra hot even mean? It's not like Starbucks can just pop it in the microwave for an extra twenty seconds. No, what you're really telling the barista is "Don't let my coffee sit around after you make it". I think that goes without saying personally.

April gets up to the register and orders, "One Grande Vanilla Latte – Extra Hot." Okay, just under the limit, she passes. One unnecessary modifier but it doesn't cross into high maintenance territory. I once took a date for some coffee and she ordered a Grande Cappuccino extra hot, upside down, with room. I bolted right away. She never even knew what happened.

April and I take a seat at a high top in the corner. Chewy dutifully lies down under my chair as any good punk biker service dog would. I take a sip of my extremely normal Grande Latte. Nothing extra, nothing modified. Just as the Starbucks Siren intended.

"Jake, I've got to ask. Why is Chewy dressed up like a gay biker dude?"

Chewy: What's a gay biker dude?

"Chewy thinks it's cool and he hates the typical doggie jacket and boots."

Chewy: That shit is for foo-foo dogs.

"At first glance, I could swear he was wearing chaps."

Chewy: I'm not wearing no chaps. What the hell are chaps?

"I briefly considered getting him those to complete the outfit, but I was afraid they'd be a little too much."

"Good call. So, this outfit was a scaled down version then?"

I can't help but notice this new April version of Jennifer is just as feisty as the original.

"When you're a Golden Doodle you need a little extra edge to get respect. I mean otherwise, you're basically just a four-legged teddy bear."

Chewy: That's right baby. I got some edge.

"He's got edge all right. So how about you Jake? Do you need more edge?"

I don't like where this conversation is heading. I think it's about time to take control and find out what I need to know.

"My friends would probably say no. But let's talk about you April. What do you normally do on a warm winter day in Chicago – besides walk in the park and meet strangely dressed canines?"

"I'm new here. Just moved to Chicago a few months back. I haven't found a steady job yet. Normally I bar tend, but this time of year the bar crowd is sparse."

"That's cool. Tell me how you make your favorite martini."

"Chill the martini glass with ice. Spray the glass with aerosol dry vermouth. Add two queen olives hand-stuffed with blue cheese. Shake some Kettle One hard until ice crystals form and the male customers begin to stare at your tits. Pour the super chilled vodka into the glass and top it with another spray of vermouth. Voila – the perfect martini."

"I'm getting hard just thinking about you making that. You should do very well bartending in Chicago."

"I do get good tips."

"When we met, I told you that you reminded me of someone. Did you ever teach school or live in Miami?"

"Nope. I moved here from Iowa. And kids are not my thing. How about you Jake? What do you do when you're not trolling for women with your Golden Doodle?"

"By training, I am a hurricane forecaster for the National Hurricane Center in Miami. Lately I find myself consulting for the FBI here in Chicago. It's a long story."

"Okay, that's interesting. How about relationships? Have you ever been married?"

"Never married. I've had exactly one serious relationship. She left me in Miami over a year ago."

"What did you do to piss her off?"

"Typical male stuff. I pushed too hard trying to uncover her secrets. Sometimes it's better not to know."

Chewy: Can't say I didn't warn you, bonehead.

"Yes, you do have to be careful what you wish for – sometimes you get more than you bargained for."

"Her name was Jennifer. I was very fond of her."

April laughs at that. "If that's how you express your affection, I think there could be another reason why she left."

"I think she might agree with you. She used to hate it when I told her that. Even when I reminded her that I was *very* fond of her."

"Well, that changes everything then. Being *very* fond of someone changes the whole meaning of the word."

"That's what I said!"

"No dummy it doesn't. A woman wants to hear the 'L' word not the 'F' word."

"I did love her though. I think she loved me back. Too bad I blew it, but it probably needed to end that way."

"If she truly loved you, maybe she'll come back one day."

Chewy: She has. She just doesn't know it yet.

> I've got pieces of April,
> I keep them in a memory bouquet,
> I've got pieces of April,
> It's a mornin' in May.
> - Pieces of April by Dave Loggins

# 15
# APRIL'S STORY

I'm called April and I'm new. Not exactly new – more like rebooted. You see I'm an 11th Dimensional entity with a mission to save you flat 3-Dimensionals from yourselves. It's a tough job but right now I'm between gigs.

I can't remember anything about my last gig, being rebooted and all. It must have been a doozy though if they needed to reboot me. Rebooting lets us 11th Dimensionals start fresh – uninhibited by whatever trauma we may have encountered in the past.

I know I've been around a long time in various forms. Saved a lot of people so they tell me. Apparently, I'm pretty good at what I do. Right now, I'm April Robinson, a non-exceptional small-town girl from Iowa trying to make it in the big city. And that's all I'll be until it's time to be something more. I told Jake that I am a bartender by trade. That's true in a way. You see, I pretty much get to invent myself however I want after a reboot. I thought bartending would make me a bit less boring – give me some edge as Jake would say. So now I am a bartender. Unemployed at the moment, but I won't be for long. Afterall, I just decided to be a bartender a few hours ago. Already I can make every alcoholic drink ever devised in the short history of homo sapiens. And not just the plain vanilla recipes either - the very best, most innovative ones. Suffice to say, I should pass any bartending test with flying colors in any bar anywhere. I'm not worried.

I am a bit worried about Jake, though. I think he's the reason I'm here in the first place. He's troubled. Anyone can see that. Like he has the world on his shoulders. I need to find out why.

I know that Jake's a wildcard. A loose cannon. I've been warned about him. He's got this limited ability to see the future that he doesn't always know how best to use. When he uses his ability at full force, it sends ripples through the 11th dimension. We've got to get a handle on that.

To make things even more complicated, I'm told he's also a sex crazed womanizer. That's less of an issue really. In the 11th dimension, sex is not really a thing, so it doesn't bother me. It may help me get to know him better.

And then there's his dog. He's special and not just because he rocks that biker dude outfit. I can tell he's an 11th Dimensional being like me. He must be assigned to guide Jake. I wish I could I just ask his dog what's going on, but he can't talk to me in this 3-D world.

Yep, I'm pretty sure Jake is the reason I'm here. To see if I can help this troubled, sex-crazed man with superpowers. But help him how? Usually, it's my job to guide whomever I'm here for - my Primaries I call them. So that's a given. I'm also supposed to make sure my Primary doesn't fuck anything up too badly. That means I'm going to have to get all up in his business.

I feel a strange connection to Jake, so I'm honestly looking forward to that part. Deep down in my 11th dimensional gut, I feel that Jake is a good person. He's trying to do the right thing. All the while, struggling to get over and move on from this Jennifer person, whoever she might be. I mean what kind of girl leaves someone just because he wants to know more about her? What a bitch.

Jake said he now works as a consultant to the FBI. You don't have to be a higher dimensional rocket scientist to guess that might have something to do with what's troubling him. I know the FBI tends to keep their actions confidential, so I'll probably have to use some special abilities of my own to figure out what they're up to with Jake. That should be the easy part.

The harder part will be to get close enough to Jake in order to guide him. He's obviously still in love with this Jennifer chick, so I'm guessing he doesn't want to get close with anyone. I don't have any special powers to help with that. Just the normal girl stuff. Hopefully, that will be enough.

It's a bit lonely being me. I know there's a big part of myself that I lost during the reboot. Lost memories. Lost friends. Maybe lost loves. Lots of loss. The only thing I really have is a sense of purpose and a sense of self. I know why I'm here and what I'm supposed to do. I also know what I am at a deeper level than memories and experiences. I have a core. A center, some people call it. I don't need a lifetime of experiences to tell me who I am. Unlike most of the beings that I encounter, I *know* what I am. Maybe that's my superpower.

I need to figure out how to get closer to Jake. I know he's attracted but I sense a certain hesitation. It's like he's conflicted about something and isn't sure how to proceed. I mean I practically had to tell him to ask for my phone number at the coffee shop. He did call me to go out this weekend, but he still seemed hesitant. I did some research on his likes and dislikes (yes, I can do that) to nudge him toward something fun. Turns out he likes kinky sex. Big surprise there. I did get an image of some fuzzy red handcuffs passing through his thoughts. Not sure what that means, but I bet I can use *those* to keep him interested. I wonder if he likes being tied up. I guess we'll see. Third Dimensional men are weird.

Not that the 11th dimension is all moonbeams and pennywhistles. In truth, the third dimensional world is a lot more interesting. It's wild and chaotic. Unpredictable and exciting. Not like where I'm from. In the higher dimensions, space has no meaning. We're all just connected waves of conscious energy. Nobody has a weight problem because nothing has mass. In the 3-dimensional world, mass exists as another form of energy and causes all sorts of problems. For one thing, mass requires space and time so people can make sense of it all. Inevitably, mass reverts back into energy, it's natural state. That transition happens everywhere, all the time – from stars to nuclear bombs. And mass never goes away quietly, as anyone familiar with Einstein's famous equation can attest.

The 11th dimension is quieter and a lot less exciting. Maybe that's why I spend so much of my existence here in 3-D world. At least stuff happens. At its core, the stuff that happens here is just mass changing from one location to another. Driven and perceived by those beings that have the consciousness to make sense of it. What you 3-Dimensionals perceive is not what's really there of course. Solid objects are not really solid at all. If you removed all the space between atomic nuclei and their surrounding electrons, all matter would fit nicely into your purse. What makes objects feel solid is the force (aka, energy) holding it all together. Time, space, and matter are all relative to who's perceiving them. They don't even exist unless they are perceived. The simple act of consciously observing brings particles into existence and changes their nature. You create your own reality. I'm just here to help keep a lid on that.

If you don't believe me, just look it up. You might start with the eminent physicist Niels Bohr. He once famously said "Everything we call real is made of things that cannot be regarded as real. If quantum mechanics hasn't profoundly shocked you, you haven't understood it yet." He didn't really understand it either, but at least he was closer than the rest of you.

Another aspect that I find interesting about you 3-D folks is how you think of yourselves as separate from everything and everyone. In your world, there's just you and everything else is not-you, separate and distinct. That of course is an illusion of existing in a 3-D world. The reality is that everything is connected. Nothing is truly separate. We're all just an instrument in a universal symphony where everyone plays their own sheet music without a conductor. Your part impacts the whole and the whole impacts you. Connected. The world around you is the music you collectively create. Often beautiful, sometimes not.

Any breed or size of dog may become a therapy dog, provided he has the proper temperament.
The job qualifications include friendliness, patience, and confidence in strange situations.
  - Therapy Dogs from Doggies.com

# 16
# CHEWY'S ADVICE

I have a date with April – who is both Jennifer and not Jennifer – this weekend. Honestly, I have no idea how to talk to her. On the one hand, April seems interested in me, wanting to get to know me better. On the other hand, she has no idea about our past relationship. How do I broach that subject? Even if she believed me, that doesn't mean she'd suddenly fall in love with me all over again. She'd probably just get freaked out and head for the hills. And it's not like I have tons of time to figure this out. In just a few weeks' time, much of Chicago may be radioactive dust. I'm probably going to need Jennifer / April to help me prevent that.

Maybe my dog can help. Chewy knows Jennifer the best – maybe even better than I do since they're both on the same dimensional plane.

"I've got no clue how to handle my date with April this weekend. What do you think I should do?"

"You must really be desperate if you're seeking dating advice from your dog."

"Come on Chewy, we both know you're not just a dog. How do I reconnect April with Jennifer and make her understand?"

"I think maybe you need to re-read Jennifer's letter. She pretty much told you what to do."

"I carry her letter with me. I read it all the time. It doesn't really cover this."

"She said the forces that bind the two of you together are strong. They won't be easily stopped. Remember?"

"So how does that help?"

"It means there are no wrong answers. Just be yourself. Let fate play itself out."

"Most of my life has been about twisting fate in a different direction. This doesn't seem like a good time to stop that."

"I think this might be the one time where you should just go along for the ride on that freight train of fate that you're always talking about. Maybe just try to tempt it a little in the right direction."

"That would be easier, I guess. So, you think I should just treat this as a normal date?"

"You don't have normal dates Jake. Treat this like the normal dates that *other* people have. Get to know her. Don't try to hump her right away. And whatever you do, keep those fuzzy red handcuffs in your drawer."

"I thought you said I should just be myself."

"Yeah, scratch that. Maybe it would help if you just treated her like you would Jennifer. After all, that's essentially who she is even if she doesn't know it yet. Treat her like Jennifer. Like you already know and love her. Like she loves you. I bet she'll respond to that at least on some level."

"That actually sounds like it might work. Do you think she knows anything about us? Does she even know anything about herself?"

"She knows she's an 11th dimensional entity and she knows she's here for a reason. I'm sure she knows that you are that reason, and she feels some strange attraction to you. Plus, she knows what I am too."

"I guess it's like she's still Jennifer but with short term memory loss. Kind of like amnesia."

"Something like that I guess, but more profound. April knows *what* she is but has no idea *who* she is. She has no past. It's not just you. It's everything. In a very real sense, she is a new person inventing herself as she goes."

"If she's here for me, does she know why? Does she know about the terrorists?"

"I don't know but I doubt it. She knows she needs to guide you somehow, but I doubt if she knows the specifics."

"Can't you just tell her? You know, explain everything?"

"Our communication is only one-way Jake. She can talk to me but doesn't hear my thoughts. She feels my true nature and I feel hers, but we can't have a conversation. Only you and I have that. Besides, how would it look if you let your dog tell her you love her?"

"Some spiritual guide you are. Don't you 11th dimensional entities ever talk? Maybe you should try texting or something."

"Paws remember? No fingers. When we're actually *in* the 11th dimension we're all connected all the time. Down here in flat land, things are more limited. It's like our Wi-Fi is down."

"Terrific, so now I get to be the one to tell her that I can see the future and talk to my dog. That should go over well."

"You did it once before and things turned out Okay. Just take your time. You don't have to spring everything on her all at once."

"Did you forget that terrorists are about to blow up Chicago? It's not like I can take my time with all this. She needs to know everything. And soon."

"A wise man once said, 'You can only be effective with people, not efficient'. You have time."

"Now you're reading Stephen Covey? Since when can you even read?"

"I came pre-equipped with certain things. Besides Covey is an 11th Dimensional being."

"I should have guessed that."

"You can almost tell by looking at him."

"What are you charging for these counseling sessions? I know with you there's always a price."

"It would be illegal for me to accept monetary compensation since I'm not licensed. I could use a new bed though. One that is warmer and cushier than the ones you usually get. The floors are freezing in here."

"You literally *ate* the last one I got you."

"I'd avoid those cheap made-in-China ones. They never last."

Tempting Fate

Guys are stimulated easily. They are easy to manipulate. All you have to do is wear a sexy outfit.
 - Jessica Alba

# 17
# FIRST DATE

April and I meet for lunch at Portello's – home of the Chicago Style Hotdog. I may be at a loss how to talk to an 11th dimensional date, but I do know my hotdogs. I've been pretty much everywhere, and I can tell you for a fact that Chicago has the best hotdogs on the planet. None of that stupid chili or sauerkraut that other places use. And no extras or options. Chicago Dogs are only made one way. If you order one somewhere outside Chicago and they ask you what you want on it, just leave. It won't be good.

"Ever had a Chicago Dog April?"
"Can't say I have. In Iowa it's mostly burgers and barbeque. And corn. Lots of corn."
"Well, you're in for a treat. Best hotdogs anywhere. Be sure to get them with the fries."
"I must admit when you said you were taking me for the best lunch in Chicago, I pictured something a bit different."
"Yeah, well I don't date much."
"Me neither. Maybe this is a normal first date."
"That's what I was going for – totally ordinary and normal."
"Most guys would probably shoot for exciting and memorable. Way to set yourself apart from the crowd Jake."
"Well, I didn't want to overwhelm you with excitement all at once. It's probably best we work up to that. You know, start slow and build from there. Like I said when we first met, I grow on people as they get to know me better."
"You mean like a fungus?"
"No, no. Think of the first time you hear a song that you like. Maybe the first time, you hardly notice it at all. But then, the more you hear it, the more familiar it seems, and soon you learn the title and recognize the tune. After a while, you look forward to hearing it. Pretty soon, you're humming it in your head. I'm like that."
"So, you're like a Barry Manilow song then?"
"Nobody likes Barry Manilow."

"True but it's been over forty years and people still can't get Mandy out of their heads."

"Don't do it April!"

April ignores my warning and begins singing significantly off key:
"Oh Mandy well
You came and you gave without taking
But I sent you away"

"Stop it!"

April: sings even louder –folks are staring at us over their hotdogs.

"Oh, Mandy
Well, you kissed me and stopped me from shaking
And I need you today
Oh, Mandy"

"FOR THE LOVE OF GOD – STOP!"

"Or maybe you're more like his jingles. You know like:
You deserve a break today, so get up and get away…."

"Or maybe this one:
Like a good neighbor, State Farm is there….."

"Alright, alright. I'm nothing like Barry Manilow. What you see is what you get. There's no growing. Satisfied?"

"It would have been so much easier for all of us if you'd just admitted that up front. So, is there anything about you that's remotely interesting Jake?"

This conversation sure went off the tracks fast. Looks like I've got no choice but to be myself with this girl.

"I enjoy kinky sex. Particularly the kind that involves fuzzy red handcuffs. I bet Barry Manilow never wrote a jingle about that shit."

"That's a start. Using them or wearing them?"

"Using them mostly. Although when it comes to sex, I'm fairly versatile."

"I'll just bet you are Doodle Boy. So how about outfits? Are there outfits involved?"

"Optional. Lady's choice. Definitely props though."

"Should I ask?"

"I'd rather show you. I'd been dating this kinky FBI agent and she got me the whole Fifty Shades of Grey collection. I'm still trying to figure out what they all do."

"Seems like there would need to be outfits. Did it come with outfits?"

"And what sort of outfits do you have in mind, oh curious one?"

"I'm thinking something black. For me, a black corset, stockings, heels, and bra. Maybe red undies just to mix it up."

"And for me?"

"Black leather. You know, like your dog."

"I thought you said he looked gay."

"Maybe that turns me on."

"Don't tell Chewy, he'll never let me forget it."

Just when I was about to see exactly what else turns April on, our hotdogs arrive.

"Seems like you and Chewy are pretty close. What else do you share besides your taste in leather?"

"Actually, that was mostly his idea."

"And how would you know that exactly?"

This is probably where Chewy would have advised me to proceed slowly with caution. Fuck that.

"He told me he wanted to look more sophisticated and important. Cops have leather jackets, so he liked that idea."

"He told you this?"

"Yep. Chewy talks to me."

"Does he talk to anyone else?"

"No just me. But he understands everything people say."

"What did he say about me?"

"He likes you and says you smell really good. He says I should take it slow with you."

"Telling me about your fuzzy handcuffs and your talking dog is taking it slow for you then?"

"Just because he talks, doesn't mean I always listen. Besides, Slow Jake was boring you. Hell, he was boring me."

"These hotdogs really are good. Slow Jake was right about that."

"Now that you know a little more than I intended about me, how about you April? What secrets do you have hiding in that cute little head of yours?"

"I'm just a small-town girl looking for some excitement in the big city."

"Now you're the one taking it slow. We both know there's much more to you than that. Tell me something about you that I don't already know."
"I want to see those fuzzy red handcuffs of yours."

I'm not stupid. I know she's trying to throw me off track. Trying to distract me from finding out more about her. Don't care.

"Finish your hotdog and I'll show you."
"You carry them with you?"
"That would be weird even for me. They're back at my place."
"Can we stop for outfits?"

> The world was on fire and no one could save me but you.
> It's strange what desire will make foolish people do.
> I never dreamed that I'd meet somebody like you.
> And I never dreamed that I'd lose somebody like you.
>   - Wicked Games by Chris Isaak

# 18
# APRIL'S GAME

This would be a lot easier if Jake were the one handcuffed to the bed. As it is, he has me at a bit of a disadvantage. So many distractions. Jake is all dominate with his floggers and whatnot – not to mention those hot leather pants (my idea). And I'm all in my hooker heels, stockings, and corset. It's all stupid novelty stuff but it's doing the job. I'm really getting turned on.

Jake keeps fumbling around with his new toys like he's looking for instructions or something. It's kind of adorable really. I don't think he has any idea what he's doing but it doesn't matter. Whatever he's doing seems to be working.

I'm trying to stay focused on the mission, but it's difficult. For one thing, Jake keeps getting me all excited and making me do things. And we haven't even really had sex yet.

My fuzzy brain is remembering that I had a strategy for dealing with this. I read up on this S&M stuff before our date. There is a thing called "Topping from the Bottom" which I should be doing now. It's where the submissive (me) actually controls the action by subtly giving instructions to her dominate partner. Mostly it involves begging your partner not to do the things you really want him to do. The problem is he is already doing all the things I really want him to do, and he's doing them before I even know I want them.

I really must get a handle on all this before I start telling him all my secrets. He's already made me tell him stuff that I hadn't intended. Nothing mission critical, but that may be because he hasn't asked me yet. So far, he knows what kind of sex I like best, what positions, what I like to do during sex, and what I like done to me. Nothing exactly top secret, but more than a girl typically shares – at least on the first date.

Things are starting to get out of hand. Maybe I'll just play along for a bit longer, though. For the sake of the mission. Sometimes sacrifices need to be made. This one was definitely not in the job description.

I think he's finally finished because now I am all sticky. Gradually, my head clears, and I glance over at Jake. It's the first time I've really seem him smile. It lights up the room and makes my very tired body tingle. I smile back at him. Maybe my plan to get Jake to open up to me is working. Or maybe he just thinks I'm a slut. Either way it was a fun way to spend the afternoon.

"I think I may have misjudged you Doodle Boy. You are way more interesting than you look."
"So basically, I grew on you."
"Parts of you sure did. I'm still tingling everyplace you put that thing."
"Want to go again?"
"Do I have a choice? Apparently, I just gave you a lifetime pass to have your way with me."
"There's a chance you may have been under duress when you gave that to me."
"Ya think? You made my brain is all mushy."
"In that case, I may have to take advantage of you again while you're still under my influence."
"Pretty please Jake."

Lather, rinse, repeat. This 3-D world definitely has some things going for it. I could get used to this.

"Would you mind ordering take out for dinner? I'm pretty sure I can't move."
"With pleasure my lady. But I can do better than that. I'll make us dinner. How does spaghetti and meatballs sound? I make my own balls and they're huge."
"I'll just bet they are. Sounds fabulous."

Dinner really was fabulous – particularly those giant meatballs. I teased him by licking the sauce off them before taking them into my mouth. That effectively pressed the pause button on dinner while Jake made me do the same to him. I liked dinner so much that Jake gave me his recipe.

This morning when I finally left for home, I felt much closer to Jake. Not just because of the great sex, although that certainly helped. We have an easy rapport - almost like we've known each other for years. We make each other laugh. He appreciates my relaxed, no big deal approach to sex. And I've come to appreciate his kinky side more than I ever imagined. Jake's not exactly normal and neither am I, but somehow it all works for us.

I'm no closer to learning what's troubling Jake or how to help him, but at least now the door is open. Tonight, we're having dinner again – at a real restaurant this time – and I suspect I'll learn a lot more about my kinky guy. Whatever happens, he'll probably want sex again tonight, so I'm wearing the appropriate outfit.

"If you want to keep a secret, you must also hide it from yourself."
— George Orwell, 1984

## 19
## MEET DARYL

I don't know if I even want to go out tonight. It's Friday and Ivonne will be expecting me to take her somewhere. Work was a bitch today and I'm dead tired. My project over at TRW is understaffed and behind schedule. We're never going to get that new actuator ready in time, and everyone on the project knows it. Too bad our division management people are in La La Land and fail to see it. They'll find out soon enough, I guess. I'll be okay though since I'm not in charge – just another engineer working nights and weekends to get it done.

It's not like I don't have other things going on in my life. My parents always tell me not to let my job consume me. To keep my focus on the important things in life. I do my best. Maybe I'll just take Ivonne out for pizza and call it a night. She'll probably want to stay over, and no doubt wants to get laid. Got to save some energy for that. I really shouldn't complain. Ivonne is a good girl and treats me well. Plus, she lets me do whatever I want in bed which helps relieve some stress.

My boss thinks I am an underachiever. He knows I have an undergraduate engineering degree from MIT but never went on to get my Masters. I did enroll in MIT grad school and passed most of the required courses, but I never bothered to complete my degree. It just didn't seem important to me. I learned what I needed. My parents understood.

I'm probably smarter and better educated that most of the other engineers on my team, but promotion and advancement have never been a priority for me. I like what I do. I get paid well. The work is interesting. Why do I need to take on more stress and responsibility? My boss doesn't get it, but he does appreciate my work.

Everyone knows me as Daryl Stevenson except my parents who call me by my family name. They immigrated to London back in the 60's from United Arab Emirates. They've taken me back there a few times when I was younger. It's a pretty cool place, home of the world's tallest building not to mention robot jockey camel racing. I wouldn't want to live there though. You can get arrested just for public displays of affection over there. I'm an affectionate guy, so I'd probably get in trouble!

Eventually, my parents moved to the US and settled in Chicago where I was born. They raised me with all things American. We had season tickets for the Cubs, Bears, and Bulls. I eventually became a rabid Bears fan suffering through season after season of unfulfilled expectations. My dad and I hardly ever missed a game, no matter how poorly they did. Just like most other Chicago fans. One of greatest years of my life was 1985, the year when the Bears finally won the Superbowl. I was only ten years old, but I can tell you the score of every game they played that year. And don't even get me started about the Chicago Bulls and Michael Jordan! Unbelievable. Or Unbelieva-Bull as we say in Chicago. And then to top it all off, the long-suffering Cubs finally win the World Series. You really couldn't script it any better than that.

Chicago is my hometown and my favorite city. It's true the weather could use improvement, but other than that, it's hard to beat. That's not to say it doesn't have the same core problems as all other American cities, but I've learned to set those aside for now and just focus on the positive.

My girlfriend, Ivonne is a positive. She's Polish-American and also a native Chicagoan. Plus, she's fun, and kind, and supper hot. My parents don't like her much, but they don't like anyone I date. I don't think they like American girls at all really, but they would never admit that.

My parents are quite traditional. Some might say old-fashioned. Outwardly they seem like all my other friend's parents. They're not really though. For one thing, they insist on calling me by my Arab name at home – Achmed. It means "Highly Praised" so I guess I should be honored. I'm not. Too many associations with the Jeff Dunham character – "I Kill You!" I never use that name outside the family. My parents would be horrified, but I watch Jeff Dunham on YouTube all the time. Every time he does his Achmed the Dead Terrorist routine, it cracks me up.

One thing my parents taught me is a deep appreciation for religion and culture. They made me memorize the Qur'an by age ten. Not many Americans realize it, but Muslims believe that God revealed holy books or scriptures to several of God's messengers. These include the Qur'an (given to Muhammad), the Torah (given to Moses), the Gospel (given to Jesus), the Psalms (given to David), and the Scrolls (given to Abraham). Qur'an revelations are regarded by Muslims as the sacred word of God, intended to correct any errors in previous holy books such as the Old and New Testaments. So really all the world's major religions are connected in this fundamental way. Kumbaya my friends.

Unfortunately, sometimes it's the differences that make all the difference. My parents helped me understand that there is great evil in the world and that much of that evil is driven by the old religions. Even Islam as it is currently widely practiced today, has lost its way. It is therefore our duty as true believers to restore Islam and help rid the Muslim world of any non-Muslim influences. This goal cannot be accomplished by religious wars and crusades. We already tried that for almost 300 years during the last millennium and not much changed. The only way forward is to unite the Muslim world around a common enemy and destroy that enemy from within. That's where I come in.

Long ago my dad taught me what God expected from me. Most of it is probably similar to what your parents taught you. In my case, these expectations were instilled with a bit more rigor since I was required to recite all of them in my prayers multiple times per day. I think of them as Achmed's rules and here they are:

1) Know the teachings of the Qur'an and be guided by them.
2) Be polite and avoid all confrontations.
3) Obey the laws of man unless they conflict with the laws of God.
4) Do not stand out from the crowd.
5) Become well educated.
6) Find a worthy career and give it your best efforts.
7) Stay humble.
8) Do not share your true beliefs with anyone.
9) Learn how to defend yourself.
10) Never take a wife.
11) Live and work as an ordinary American until God's will is shown to you.
12) Prepare yourself for paradise.

I believe I have lived these rules fairly well up to this point. My parents are proud of me but warn that the hardest challenges are still to come. As God's will has finally been revealed to me, I see that their warning is true.

So, I prepare myself for paradise, as time allows. Part of that preparation is to withdraw from my earthly concerns. That part is going slowly, I must admit. I'm still very invested in my job, spending most of my time trying to get my damn project back on schedule. I should start to pull back on that a bit, but it's hard. Same problem with Ivonne. I know I should end our relationship to focus on the important things, but she brings so much pleasure into my life, it's hard to give her up. Particularly since I know my remaining time here is growing short. And as much as I might want to believe there are seventy-two virgins awaiting me in paradise, I just can't get my head around that.

For one thing, I'm not sure why I want to have a virgin in the first place, much less 72 of them. That sounds like work to me – teaching all those women about sex. What am I - some sort of heavenly sex education teacher? For another thing, the Qur'an is very unclear about this aspect of paradise. There is no mention anywhere in the Qur'an of the actual number of virgins available in paradise. The number seventy-two comes from something Mohammed was overheard saying in passing. Something to the effect of: "The smallest reward for the people of paradise is an abode where there are 80,000 servants and 72 wives." Now are those wives in addition to the virgins? No one really knows. And who's going to manage those 80,000 servants? Not me, I hope. I can barely handle one girlfriend and a small project team. Plus, there is some disagreement whether the Qur'an even mentions virgins at all. Some scholars believe the word "hur", which occurs four times in the Qur'an, should be translated as "virgin". But others believe it is more correctly translated as "maiden with dark eyes". Personally, I would prefer the latter, but I guess I'll see soon enough.

Honesty is such a lonely word,
Everyone is so untrue,
Honesty is hardly ever heard,
And mostly what I need from you.
— Honesty by Billy Joel

# 20
# THE CONFRONTATION

Tonight will be our third date. April and I are getting along fine, and the sex is great. Our communication however is lacking. She wants to know all about me but continues to be evasive whenever I ask anything about her. Tonight, that will end one way or another. There's no time to be coy. If April is who I think she is, I'll need her help to save Chicago.

I'm taking April to one of the more famous restaurants in Chicago, The Berghoff. It's German and while it's not exactly Octoberfest, April has been saying she wants to see what classic Chicago dining is all about. The Berghoff has been around over one hundred years, so I think it qualifies. Plus, I like the Sauerbraten and the root beer.

I arrange a quiet table for two so we can talk. There is much to discuss and little time for pleasantries.

"What do you think of this place?"
"It's exactly how I pictured old-world Chicago! I can't wait to try the Wiener Schnitzel."
"I think you tried that on our last date."
"Funny man. I didn't realize your dick was German."
"There's a whole butt load of things we don't know about each other April. Maybe we should fix that. Tonight would be good."

Nothing like diving right in. We're far from the shallow now as Lady Gaga would say.

"I'm a private person Jake. It takes me awhile to open up to people."
"That doesn't stop you from asking all kinds of questions about me. Come on April, every time I ask anything about your life, you shut me out. You're obviously hiding more than a few secrets."
"A lady is entitled to her secrets Jake."
"You guard them like a high security prison. If you want a relationship with me, that's not going to cut it."
"Well then, maybe I deserve a good spanking."

"Don't try to distract me. We both know you enjoy that too much anyway."

"Just like your beach babes, right Jake?"

"How would you know anything about that?"

"You have quite the reputation."

"What are you, my stalker?"

"You wish."

"I know some stuff about you too April."

"Like what?"

"I know you're not what you seem to be. There's a lot more going on with you than you care to admit. Much more."

"Now who's the stalker? What do you think you know Jake?"

"I know exactly who and what you are April. More than you do apparently."

"How can you say that? We've practically just met."

"And yet you certainly seem to know a few things about me. What else do you think you know about me besides my affinity for beach babes?"

"I know you're a wildcard. That you can do things that no human should be able to do. You can see the future."

"And I know you are an 11th dimensional being. Trying to save the world from people like me."

Bam! That knocked her off balance. For the first time in our short history together, April looks uncomfortable. She stares at me with a wide-eyed glare.

"How could you possibly know that? Wait, did you peek into my future?"

"Nope. More like your past."

"I'm new. I don't have a past."

"Well then. I guess I know a little bit more about you than you know about me."

"I very much doubt that. What do you think you know about me Jake?"

"I know you are good. Super extra good. But you're no angel. Aside from your enjoyment of kinky sex, you are also evasive and annoying."

"Look who's talking. You have a whole closet full of sex toys and you have private conversations with your dog."

"Do you really want to know who you are April?"

"I know who I am, thank you. But I am curious who you think I am."

"It's easier to just show you. Go ahead and read my mind now. I know you can do it. I give you my permission."

I shift my thoughts towards some of my favorite memories of Jennifer and me together. The time when we met. The times she saved me and my friends. The day she told me who she really was.

A few minutes pass as I fondly recall my life with Jennifer. April looks increasingly uncomfortable.

"Those are some lovely memories, Jake. Your ex-girlfriend seems nice and all, but I don't understand what that has to do with me."

"Did you see what she was?"

"She's an 11th dimensional spirit like me. It doesn't surprise me. Apparently, you need a lot of supervision."

"Not just *like* you. She *is* you."

That got her attention. She's starting to squirm in her chair.

"That's ridiculous. How could you possibly know that?"

"Chewy told me, and in your heart, you know it's true."

"Well, isn't that convenient? Your dog told you. The one who can only talk to *you*."

"Chewy remembers your smell. He says you smell super extra good, and he can always tell when you're nearby."

"So, you're basing all this on something your dog told you. Excuse me if I have my doubts."

"Maybe you should read this. It's the last thing Jennifer wrote to me before she left."

I always carry Jennifer's note with me. I feel like it connects me to her somehow. Until April showed up, it was the only connection I had. Now I hand it over to this new version of Jennifer so she can finally see the truth.

*My Dearest Jake,*

*The word 'sorry' doesn't feel right. I'm not sorry for my actions. I did what I knew in my heart was the right thing. We both did. There were consequences and most of them were wonderful – even miraculous. That's a word I don't use lightly. What most people call miraculous, I think of as normal. What makes this truly miraculous is that we achieved together what neither of us could do on our own. Something I hadn't even known was possible.*

*But you knew. You saw that by combining our special abilities and mixing them with human science and ingenuity, we could change the inevitable. That's your real gift – not just your limited ability to see the future. I am so proud of you Jake. You saved us all.*

*The price for that is us. In the big picture, that's hardly anything. To me, it's everything and I know it is for you as well. It saddens me beyond words. You probably think of me as a girl with a mission – some kind of higher power. There's no denying it, I am all of that. But right now, at this moment, I am a girl who loves you more than life. And I am heartbroken.*

*We shall never see each other again Jake. That's the price I paid for helping you derail that freight train of fate. The price we both paid. I know you. You're going to want to solve this. You're going to move heaven and earth to find me. Please don't. It will just cause you more pain. You can't find me. Where I'm going you cannot follow.*

*Let me leave you with this thought. Maybe it will give you some comfort and even a bit of solace. You will never again see the girl you knew as Jennifer, but we will meet again. I don't know where or when. You won't know me, and I won't know you. But we will feel a connection. The forces that bound our spirits together originally are strong and eternal. Just like that freight train, they won't be easily stopped. In the meantime, keep Chewy close. Listen to him. He will guide you back to me.*

*Goodbye my love. Just remember, I'll be seeing you.*

*Yours always,*
*Jennifer*

For a long while, April stares blankly at the note and says nothing. I watch as the truth about her past and the true nature of our relationship gradually washes over her. Her shoulders begin to shake, and tears form in her eyes. I get up from my chair hug her silently. She starts to cry softly into my shoulder.

We stay like that for a long time. Neither of us says a word, but for the first time we are really communicating. Sometimes there are no words.

Finally, April squeezes my hand showing me she's ready.

"Am I really her?"

"Yes and no. You are the essence of Jennifer. But with a twist that's all your own April. For whatever time we have left, I plan to discover all your twists and turns."

"What by tying me to your bed?"

"That could be one way. I have others."

"Tell me more about me first."

"You have no idea how much I've been wanting to do that."

Tempting Fate

"Those who cannot remember the past are condemned to repeat it."
— George Santayana

# 21
# THE HISTORY LESSON

After dinner, I take April back to my place so we can talk in private. She's trying to act stoic, but I can tell she's just hanging on by a thread. I need to tread lightly now, but there's more she needs to know. Much more.

"Maybe I should just give you the headlines first and then you can ask questions to fill in the blanks."

"Okay Jake but tell me all of it."

"We met while we were living in Miami. I was a hurricane forecaster for the National Hurricane Center, and you were a high school science teacher. Your name was Jennifer Ortega. You were the oldest daughter from a Cuban family also living in Miami."

"Do you have a picture of her - slash me?"

"Here's one from when we first met. I was walking Chewy in the park, and you walked up to us in your yellow short-shorts and tank top."

"I was pretty hot."

"And Chewy thought you smelled really good. Anyway, you walked over to pet my dog and told me to call you later so you could play with Chewy. We went out for coffee."

"That's pretty close to how we met."

"Those who cannot remember the past are condemned to repeat it."

"That's one way to look at it. It's more likely that your pickup techniques haven't changed much."

"Either way, I picked you up *twice* Angel Baby."

"As you said, I'm no angel. Keep going."

"Six months later, you moved in with me. Things were going fine but you could tell something was bothering me. Until I met you, I had used my rather modest abilities to see twelve minutes into the future for the sole purpose of having sex with as many women as possible. After I met you, I began to feel guilty that I was wasting this powerful gift – at least not using it for the betterment of mankind. I couldn't talk about it with you because I hadn't told you yet – I was afraid you would think I was nuts. So, I kept everything to myself until you forced my hand."

"How did I do that?"

"You told me you were going to leave me if I didn't tell you what was going on. When I finally did tell you, you pretended you didn't believe me. Made me prove it to you. Later I realized you were just pretending in order to protect your own secrets – about which I knew nothing at the time."

"Did things get better between us once you told me the truth?"

"At first they did. In fact, you helped me expand my abilities by showing me how to trust my instincts and focus my mind. You helped me discover that I could also see other people's futures besides my own if I wanted. Eventually I was able to see future world events up to twelve days into the future. And even sometimes change those events, although not very reliably."

"That's amazing Jake. Were you able to use your new powers for the betterment of mankind thing?"

"Eventually yes. I'd always been frustrated by the limitations of only being able to see twelve minutes into the future. I wanted to use my ability to better predict hurricanes, but with only a twelve-minute advanced notice that was impossible. But once I was able to see major world events twelve *days* into the future, it became possible for me to really do some good in the world."

"What kind of good?"

"I concentrated my efforts on predicting hurricanes. Our computer models at the time were notoriously bad at predicting the strength and track of a hurricane more than five days out. Even up to a few days before landfall, those models were often significantly wrong causing either unnecessary deaths or unnecessary evacuations. My new abilities changed all that. I could see exactly where the hurricanes would end up twelve days into the future."

"But how did that help? Who would believe you?"

"Exactly the problem. Plus, I was too afraid to do anything that might change the future for fear of making it worse. That's when you suggested the concept of a "morally unambiguous" intervention."

"I guess I had a larger vocabulary back then. What the hell does that mean?"

"It means that if the future event I see is so terrible, so deadly, then *anything* I do to change that outcome must be better."

"Did you encounter some of those events?"

"Yes, but I decided to stick strictly to what I knew best, hurricanes. Now that I think about it, it was you who suggested that. We figured that trying to intervene into the unknown territory of other world events would not go well. At least with hurricanes, I knew pretty much everything there was to know about them."

"What happened?"

"The first time was with Hurricane Jake – don't laugh, I don't name them – a few years back. It was going to form into the worse kind of hurricane, a Category 5, and hit downtown Jacksonville. Thousands would die. So, I intervened. I chose an alternative outcome where the hurricane goes harmlessly out to sea. That's when I found out the significant limitations of my newfound power. Changing a major world event -I call them Mega Events – is like shuffling a deck of cards. I may change the outcome, but I can never be sure what I am changing it to. Instead of hitting Jacksonville with an 85% probably as a Category 5 storm, the future changed to a crap shoot between three almost equally probable events. One was the go harmlessly out to sea thing, but the others had it striking either Jacksonville or Miami. That's when I got my big idea.

"Sounds like you were pretty fucked to me."

"That's exactly what Jennifer said. I won't bore you with the details, but I found a way to use these alternative futures to calibrate the computer model we used. I made it so that the computer was forecasting exactly the possible outcomes that I saw in my head. That made the model deadly accurate. Our newly enhanced computer model correctly predicted that Hurricane Jake would hit just south of Jacksonville. We had the forecast in time to evacuate the low-lying areas and only a few lives were lost. So basically, your boyfriend prevented what would have been the worst natural disaster in US history."

"So now you're my boyfriend? When did that happen?"

"A long time ago, and I'm way more than that April. You may not feel it yet, but I'm really hoping you will."

"I feel it Jake. I'm just trying to get my head around all this."

"Moving on. Later, one of my colleagues at the National Hurricane Center discovered my unauthorized changes to his computer model and confronted me. Fortunately, he is also my best friend so when I told him about my abilities, he decided to help me. Together we developed a secret backdoor program and added it to the computer forecasting model. Now whenever I see a hurricane coming twelve days out, I can just call him with the data, and he can plug it into the model. That makes his hurricane forecast more accurate by a factor of ten."

"That's all well and good but how did you fuck things up with Jennifer?"

"I blame my lizard brain."

"Your what?"

"That's the part of our brain that reacts instinctively to patterns we might not otherwise notice. I began to see that Jennifer knew things that she shouldn't know. And then I began to suspect that she was doing things that no human could do."

"Like what?"

"Saving my life mostly. And my friends. Once from lightning at a backyard barbeque and once on a sailing trip back to Miami."

"So, it bothered you that your girlfriend was saving your life?"

"It bothered me that she tried to keep that part of herself hidden from me. You know just like you tried to do?"

"Ouch."

"Eventually it bothered me so much that I looked into her future to see what I could find out. It was something I'd promised her that I'd never do. Turns out she was on to me and punched me in the face before I could see anything."

"I totally would have done that. I must still have a lot of Jennifer in me."

"No doubt. Anyway, that pissed her off so bad that she agreed to tell me the truth. But not before warning me there would be consequences. I ignored her warning and she told me. Then she broke up with me and moved out."

"That sounds kind of harsh."

"I really didn't give her much choice. Knowing the truth about her drove me crazy. I couldn't accept what she was. Eventually, she gave up and left. She even took Chewy away from me. Said he had been reassigned. I still had my dog, but he wasn't Chewy anymore. Plus, she even reset me – whatever that means."

"I bet that taught you not to piss off 11th dimensional women."

"You'd think so, but I am a slow learner. She just moved down the street from me and we stayed friends. Eventually she even gave me Chewy back – saying I needed someone to keep an eye on me."

"I thought you said she left you permanently?"

"Eventually she did, but we got back together first. I drove up to Orlando to surprise her while she was attending a teacher's conference. I was making some good progress in my research to improve our hurricane forecasting model, so I was feeling hopeful. As I drove up, I checked the Mega Event Stream and was shocked to see there was a major fire going to happen at Jennifer's hotel within a few hours. I drove like a madman and got there just before the fire started. I was able to rescue her just as the fire broke out. She was so grateful that she agreed to move back in with me."

"Way to save the day Jake! Did you guys have wild sex?"

"Normally I'd never kiss and tell but since she is you, I guess it's okay. I hadn't had sex since Jennifer left, so I kept her in bed for the next three days. I didn't even stop to let her unpack her bags."

"So how did you manage to fuck that up? *Again?*"

"This time it was totally not my fault. Just circumstances conspiring against us. The perfect storm if you will. Literally. Things were going great between us and then Jennifer started acting weird. There was something big upsetting her and she didn't want to tell me. After a few hours with Mr. Fuzzy Red Handcuffs, she told me what was wrong. Turns out Jennifer gets premonitions when there's anything happening in the near future that might hurt me. That's how she saved me from the lightning and the boating accident. This time the event was too big even for me to stop. That's why she didn't want to tell me. There was nothing we could do. She had foreseen that the force of fate in this case would be too powerful for my limited abilities to change the future. In sixty days' time, a killer super hurricane was going to hit Florida and destroy every major city on the peninsula. It would be by far the worst natural disaster in recorded history, and nothing could stop it. The only way to survive it would be to move out of state.

"Holy crap."

"That's what I said. And in the ultimate universal irony, they named it after you – well Jennifer actually."

"What did you do? I think I would have just made sure to get my family and friends out of harm's way."

"We did that – gave Jennifer's family an all-expense paid vacation to Chicago. I got Jennifer a refundable ticket to join them, but I wanted to try something first. My team and I had been working to identify the exact initial conditions that spark hurricane formation. I had gone out on a research mission earlier that year to track those tropical waves coming off Africa that eventually spin up into hurricanes. Our research discovered that the physics of tropical depression formation – the first stage of a hurricane – is very precarious. The conditions need to be exactly right. If anything is even a tiny bit off, they won't form at all – at least not at that place and time."

"I don't understand how that helps."

"It was all purely theoretical, but we had the brainpower and resources on our forecasting team to give it a try. The idea was to use our newfound knowledge on hurricane formation along with my detailed twelve-day peek at the future to estimate the exact location where this super hurricane would begin to form. Then we could use one of our research vessels to head out to that location and try to disrupt the formation."

"So, your plan was to go hundreds of miles out to sea where a super hurricane is about to form in order to try to stop it? I'm no expert but that sounds completely insane."

"That's pretty much what my team said when I first introduced the idea. Fortunately, one of the members of that team was my good friend Phil who had helped me build the backdoor to our forecasting model. He already knew firsthand about my power to predict the future and believed me when I told him about Hurricane Jennifer. Between the two of us - the three of us really because Jennifer was there to back me up - we convinced the team this was really going to happen unless we could do something to stop it."

"How in the world could you hope to stop something like that? I thought hurricanes were the most powerful forces in nature."

"They are and there was no way we could really stop it. But with just the right plan and a lot of luck, I thought we might be able to nudge it a little. Even a small change in the initial condition of a storm can drastically change its intensity and course. You know like the famous Butterfly Effect?"

"What was the plan? To get out in front of the storm and flap your wings?"

"Not exactly. We planned to use rice bran oil. About a hundred drums of the stuff. Spread exactly at the right time and place ahead of the tropical wave just as its about to start spinning into a tropical depression. In theory, if we did it just right, it could lower the ocean surface temperature and evaporation rate just enough to delay storm formation."

"Just to summarize, nothing like that had ever been tried before and even if it worked, at best it would only delay the hurricane formation a bit, not stop it. Do I have that right?"

"All true. But we all thought it was worth a try - given the alterative. You know – the morally unambiguous decision."

"But wasn't it dangerous for all of you to be out there while the largest hurricane in history was forming?"

"As it turned out yes. That tropical wave we were following was more intense than usual. Tropical waves are a bit like a line of scattered thunderstorms on land. Sometimes not so bad, other times, really bad. This one was so bad that it slowed our progress towards the calculated drop point. After several hours at full speed on our research ship, it become clear we were never going to make it in time. We were still about 400 miles away from our destination when I called you via satellite phone to give you the bad news."

"What happened? I don't remember anything about Florida being destroyed by a hurricane."

"You saved the day. You transported our vessel and all its contents 400 miles west in an instant. We had time to spread the oil before the tropical wave arrived and it worked. Our little trick with the oil had delayed the formation of the tropical depression by about two days. That was enough to significantly alter the path and intensity of the storm. Eventually Hurricane Jennifer hit Cocoa Beach, Florida as a strong Category 2 hurricane. Property damage and loss of life was minimal."

"Oh my god. That's incredible. I didn't even know I could do something like that."

"Well technically you can't. it's against the rules. On our satellite phone call, you warned me there would be consequences. You wanted to do it anyway. Millions of lives were at stake. By the time I returned home, you were gone, leaving me only the note I showed you."

"Jake I'm so sorry. I had no idea. You must have been completely devastated. I guess I was too. It hurts when I think about it. I feel like my past was stolen from me, along with my heart."

"You were the love of my life. I'm not sure *I* could have sacrificed that – even to save all those people. But you never hesitated. I told you – you are super extra good."

That's when April finally lost her stoic composure and started to cry. I guess the weight of it all was just too much. Part of me felt terrible for making her relive such painful events. But another, more selfish part of me, was relieved. Jennifer had found her way back to me.

That was enough history for one evening. We spent the rest of the night hugging each other in the dark. Grieving for what we had lost but also looking toward the future with newfound hope.

Tempting Fate

I was born here and I'll die here against my will,
I know it looks like I'm moving, but I'm standing still,
Every nerve in my body is so vacant and numb,
I can't even remember what it was I came here to get away from,
Don't even hear a murmur of a prayer,
It's not dark yet, but it's getting there.
— Not Dark Yet by Bob Dylan

# 22
# CLOSING IN

Chewy and I are out every day now canvassing a thirty square-mile area west of downtown. Our intelligence sources indicate this is the most likely location where the bomb is being constructed. The area is chock full of warehouses and other buildings suitable for such an endeavor. It would take an entire army to search, and we don't have one of those at our disposal. The best Chewy and I can do is sniff out any persons we encounter looking for suspects. Agent Toomey gives us a new grid search map every day for us to focus our efforts.

We did make some progress thwarting Kevin Healy's fuse acquisition activities. The FBI raided the arms supplier that Kevin planned to contact and confiscated whatever was stored in their facility. No fuse of the kind Healy was looking to acquire was found. No doubt it was stored off-site. The FBI is now interrogating the arms dealer and his staff, but so far, they have not revealed anything useful. It is entirely possible the Kevin Healy deal already went down as word of the raid got out. Toomey thinks the terrorists now have their fuse.

Whatever might have happened with the fuse, the terrorist network now must be aware that the FBI is closing in. Taking down one of their key suppliers would be a dead giveaway. SIGINT reports that all suspicious communication activity in the area has gone dark. Whatever communication that occurs between cell members now will likely be limited to low tech dead drops. We are still waiting for Healy to contact the communications lead for his cell. Once he does that, we should be able to make real progress.

Fortunately for the city of Chicago, it's not just Chewy and I searching for the bomb site location. Agent Toomey has drones in the air twenty-four-seven covering the target area. Some of those drones have high resolution video cameras that capture the image of anyone walking or driving through the area. Facial recognition programs are constantly humming away back at headquarters uncovering the identity of all those individuals. Other drones are carrying magnetometers which can identify any large metallic objects within the target area buildings. Still other drones have sensitive radiation detectors which can identify any radiation source even slightly above the normal background radiation. So far, all this technology has come up empty.

I'm checking the Mega Event Stream headlines every day now for any news of terrorist activity or, worse case, any news of Chicago being vaporized in the next twelve days. Everything has been quiet so far.

Tonight, I need to tell Jennifer / April (Jenapril?) what's happening and see if she can help somehow. That will completely violate my security clearance, and I would be arrested for treason if anyone found out. But my instincts tell me sacrifices will have to be made if we hope to save my hometown. One of those sacrifices may have to be me. I hope not. It would be just my luck to get vaporized or executed right after finding Jennifer again.

While I am contemplating that ultimate universal irony, we get word that Healy is making another dead drop. Agent Toomey has us picked up by a surveillance van within minutes. We get just close enough so I can take a look at Healy's immediate future. He's going to leave a message for his communication lead confirming delivery of the fuse and warning him about the intense FBI presence. This one will be a double-blind drop. Two cutouts will be used, and Healy doesn't know either one. Fabulous.

The initial drop location is under a US mailbox near the corner of Cicero and W. Madison St. We can take a different route now that we know where he's going. We get there before him and watch as Healy expertly drops his cigarette carton near the mailbox. While bending over to pick them up with one hand, he uses the other hand to reach under the mailbox and place his message. The whole thing took less than two seconds. Unless you were watching him closely with high powered binoculars like we were, you'd have absolutely no idea that anything suspicious was happening.

After several hours of surveillance and several pizza slices, the first cutout arrives to fetch the message. This one is no innocent college student. He's far too skilled at this. He pretends to drop the letter he's mailing and then snatches up the message along with his letter. He mails his letter and walks away to his car parked a short distance away. We follow his car in our van. He drives to another mailbox across town and drops another envelope into the box. It no doubt contains the original message and is probably addressed to the second cutout. Now it is mixed up with hundreds of other pieces of US mail along with the appropriate postage, no doubt. Very clever. Unless we break into the mailbox and open all the contents (a major violation of all kinds of federal laws) we'd have no idea where the message was being sent. Fortunately, the FBI wasn't born yesterday. Shortly after Healy made his initial dead drop, one of our equally expert agents dropped his glasses near the mailbox and attached a microscopic tracking device to the message. Now all we have to do is wait for the post office to deliver it. In the unlikely event that the letter is being sent out of town, it'll go to a central processing center, and we'll get a court order to intercept it to see where it's addressed. More likely it is being sent to a location very nearby and will be delivered tomorrow.

Sure enough, it's delivered the next day to a residential mailbox in a brownstone apartment building on the North Side. We make careful note of exactly which apartment box contains the letter and wait. As we expected, the apartment is currently unoccupied and is being advertised for lease. Before long, a young man on a bicycle arrives and opens the box. He's from a local courier service based on his jacket logo. We follow him several blocks until he stops in front of a private residence and slides the envelop under the front door without ringing the bell. With luck, this will be the home of our target – the communication lead of Healy's acquisition cell.

Within minutes, we have our answer. The house belongs to a forty-three-year-old man named Harvey Slayton. According to DMV records, Harvey has lived at that address for five years and owns a 2015 Buick LaCrosse. Within seconds we use his picture and social security number to dive deeper into his identity. Harvey Slayton's real name is Kareem Musaffa. He immigrated to the US with his family over twenty years ago from Pakistan. No one in his family has a criminal record, but his uncle has been linked to various al-Qaeda operatives. It sounds like we have our guy.

Now the question is what we do with that information. One approach would be to pick him up for questioning. It is very likely he knows his counterpart in the Operations Cell – the cell putting the bomb together. Getting that information out of him will take some time -at least here in the United States where "enhanced" interrogation methods are illegal. None of us are sure we have that much time.

So, we go with Plan B. I'll wait until he comes out to grab his evening paper or something and get a read on his immediate future. Maybe I'll get lucky, and he'll be planning something nefarious in the next twelve minutes. Worse case, I'll tune into his wavelength and be able to keep checking on his future over the next few days. In the meantime, the FBI will investigate every associate, every phone call, and every text message that Harvey, aka Kareem, has made over the last five years. Our best hope is that he will attempt to contact his communications counterpart in the operations cell. If he does that, we should be able to roll up the entire terrorist network within a few days and prevent a very unpleasant Springtime in Chicago.

Khalid ibn al-Walid joined Muhammad and participated in various expeditions for him. Khalid once reported that the fighting was so intense during one battle, that he broke nine swords. This earned him the title 'Saif-ullah' meaning "The Sword of Allah".
Khalid is said to have fought around a hundred battles, both major battles and minor skirmishes as well as single duels, during his military career. Having remained undefeated, he is claimed by some to be one of the finest military generals in history.
— Description from Museum Replicas Limited - Sword of Khalid ibn Walid

# 23
# JIHAD IS HARD

I quit my job today. I've been working at TRW for ten years and they feel like family. The project I'm working on really needs my help, and we've all been working long hours to try to get back on schedule. My boss was flabbergasted. It's the worst possible time for me to leave. Not that they can't replace me, there's plenty of qualified engineers who would love to work for TRW. But there's an old axiom in project management – adding personnel to a late project makes it later. I wasn't the one in charge of the project, but I was the key go-to person. It's going to be very difficult for them to replace me at this point. Impossible really. The project will undoubtably suffer and there is no one to blame but me.

I told everyone that my mother had suddenly taken ill, and I needed to look after her full time. It's a bad omen to say something like that, but my mother understood. It was necessary for the cause.

Of course, my boss and my other team members felt differently. It's customary in this country to just hire someone to take care of one's aging parents. Or to put them in some kind of senior's home. That's not how we do it where I'm from, but I couldn't make them understand that. In the end, I just had to pack up and leave without any goodbye parties or fanfare. Daryl Stephenson has left the building.

For the perfect end to a shitty day, my next stop was my girlfriend, Ivonne's place. It was time. God's mission is now all consuming and there is no time to play with my girlfriend. I needed to break up with her, and there was no way my sick mother routine was going to work this time. It's difficult because Ivonne has never given me any reason to leave. She's pretty much the perfect girlfriend. She's understanding of my long hours at work. She never quizzes me on where I've been or what I've been doing. She's always happy to see me whenever I can spare the time. I can't think of a single excuse to break up with her. My only choice is to be mean about it, so she gets the message and doesn't try to change my mind. I hate doing that. She doesn't deserve it - aside from being an infidel and everything. My parents would happily cause her harm for that reason alone, but I'm not that way. It's one thing for me to blow up a bunch of nameless, faceless, and godless people. It's quite another to be cruel to someone I know and care about. It would be easier for me to just kill her, but I can't risk that kind of attention.

So instead, I went over to her place and just told her straight out that I never wanted to see her again. I told her she was a worthless bitch, and I could no longer stand the sight of her. Her immediate reaction was stunned silence, so I took advantage of that pause in the drama to walk out the door. As I slammed the door behind me, I heard her start to cry. My cruelty is probably going to fuck up her trust in men for quite some time, but God Willing, she's going to get vaporized by the bomb soon anyway. No time for regrets. I've got shit to do.

The FBI is closing in on us. My Acquisitions Cell has been compromised. We can no longer depend on them for any more materials. Fortunately, we already have most of what we need. The rest should be just ordinary things we can get from Home Depot.

Originally our plan was to explode the bomb on Laylat al-Qadr, The Night of Destiny. That's the night when the Qur'an was first sent down from Heaven to the world. It's also the night when the first verses of the Qur'an were revealed to the prophet Muhammad. How glorious that we might enlighten the godless world on the anniversary of Muhammed's enlightenment.. Unfortunately, Laylat al-Qadr falls at the end of April this year and we may not be able to wait that long.

Unlike my project at TRW, this one - we call it "The Sword of Allah" - is progressing like clockwork. Originally the planners back in Syria wanted to name it "The Torch that Lights A Thousand Souls" but we vetoed that. Something like that may work back there, but it doesn't exactly roll off the tongue around here. We needed something that would fit better in a headline for the Chicago Tribune and the New York Times. Not to mention Twitter.

It's now the first week in April and our scheduled detonation date is April 28th. I can speed that up by several days if I need to, but we need to be careful. Assembling an atomic bomb, even our rudimentary version, is tricky business. For one thing, it's not a good idea to assemble it into a working bomb until you're ready to use it. Like all bombs, they tend to want to explode once you put all the parts together. Plus, the assembly process is very delicate. Everything must be put together with extreme precision. We have the skills to do that, but it takes time to do it right. One mistake and boom! And not the kind of boom we want either – just the normal explosive kind. And even once we assemble the bomb, we need several hours to calibrate it. Small variations in temperature, humidity, and air pressure can fuck up the whole thing.

Suffice to say the bomb needs to be carefully adjusted for maximum explosive impact. The scientists tell us that if we do this right, we should be able to create about a 20-kiloton blast. That's slightly larger than the bomb that destroyed Hiroshima. It would be enough to destroy most of downtown and kill about 150,000 people almost instantly. Another 200,000 would be severely injured – and most of them would die within a few years – Praise God.

I am honored to be the one chosen to push the detonation button and therefore the first one to die in the glorious Sword of Allah. The rest of the assembly team will be standing a few meters away, so I'll beat them to paradise by about 0.01 millionths of a second.

But we can no longer wait until the end of April. Our Night of Destiny will have to be sooner. The FBI is too close. I'll need to pull the team together one last time to discuss options.

The power of the commercial was originally thought to lie in its subtle justification of the fact that [L'Oréal] Preference cost ten cents more than [rival Clairol's] Nice 'n Easy. But it quickly became obvious that the last line was the one that counted. On the strength of 'Because I'm worth it,' Preference began stealing market share from Clairol.
— Malcolm Gladwell in a 1999 article for the New Yorker

# 24
# BECAUSE YOU'RE WORTH IT

Making a crude nuclear device can be tricky but the technology is decades old and well understood. Any first-year engineering student would understand the basic principles involved. By the time they graduated, they could probably even build one given access to the right materials and resources. It's not rocket science as they say.

The complications occur mostly in gaining access to the "right" nuclear material. Fortunately for our little team, there is lots of wiggle room for exactly what "right" means when it comes to building a bomb – at least a crude one like we're making. When countries like Russia and the United States build a nuclear bomb, their specs call for highly enriched uranium, somewhere around 90% pure U-235. That allows them to precisely control the yield, reliability, and size of the bomb. That stuff is really hard to make and even harder to get your hands upon.

God Willing, we can make a crude version of the same bomb using much less enriched uranium – somewhere in the neighborhood of 20% pure U-235. And there's tons of that stuff lying around. Literally. There's about twenty-three hundred tons of enriched uranium worldwide in stockpiles from 40 different countries stored in hundreds of different buildings. Such uranium is relatively easy to handle and not all that radioactive. And occasionally some of it goes missing.

Now beggars can't be choosy, so the uranium we get comes in various forms and purities and is often mixed in with other stuff. That would make a difference to someone who was designing bombs to fit in warheads and airplanes. But not so much for our purposes. The planners back home did some rudimentary purification, such as separating out any extraneous metals and changing any uranium oxide back into metallic form. But for the most part, our solution is just to use more of the stuff. Basically, the less enriched and pure the uranium, the more of it you need to make it go boom. That adds significant size and weight to the bomb, but since we're not planning to move it anywhere, we don't really care.

We were able to acquire about 300 pounds of medium enriched uranium for our little project. We estimate it is about 50% pure U-235, far below what is considered weapons grade by today's standards, but we have about three times more of it than is theoretically required to achieve critical mass for a nuclear explosion. All we have to do is to smash it all together in just the right way for just the right amount of time. Not only that, but uranium is so dense that this whole amount can fit in about three one-gallon gas cans, Praise God. Of course, we use far more gas cans than that – bad things tend to happen when you cram too much uranium together. I've no desire to experience premature detonation like my namesake Jeff Dunham character. Don't laugh - I KILL YOU!

We now have all the required components ready for assembly in our little warehouse just west of downtown. The lease was executed by a shell company owned by an offshore holding company which is a wholly owned subsidiary of an international cosmetics company – the one that says, "Because You're Worth It!". And you are.

Our original plan was to complete assembly about two weeks from now. Assembly takes one week and is very delicate, precise work. We would then spend the remaining few days calibrating the bomb before the Night of Destiny. Once we enter the assembly phase, our Quiet Period begins. No communication is sent within or between cells. All we do is wait and watch for any threats that might impact our plans.

Now we need to move that up. Assembly must begin this week. There are still a few more minor components that need to be precured but nothing major. Our assembly team is tired, but they are ready, God Willing. But this is a major change and requires the entire team to be onboard – lots of moving parts to coordinate. I need to gather all the necessary team members to work round the clock at the bomb site. This will involve some risk with the FBI so close, but it is necessary.

Our security is tight. There is only one person on earth who knows how to contact the other members of our operations team. But that's all he knows. He doesn't know their identities. And I don't even know his identity, he is only known to me as Chris. In order to contact Chris with a message for the team, I need to contact Anton, who only knows two things about our operation. He knows me and he knows how to contact Chris. That's the extent of his involvement. Within just a few hours, I've drafted an encoded message for the team and delivered it to Anton. Chris should have the message (which he is completely unable to read) within another few hours. It will take another day for Chris to deliver the message to all the other team members. Unbeknownst to Chris, one of the team members receiving the message knows to send a receipt confirmation to me since I am not a recipient of my own message. If I do not receive that receipt confirmation, I'll know that Chris has been compromised.

So far everything has gone pretty much according to plan. The FBI was able to compromise someone in our Acquisitions Cell but nobody in that cell knows anything about our mission or any of the people in our Operations Cell. Their role had already been accomplished before the FBI closed in, so there is no need to communicate with them further. I'm sorry for their loss, but it's all for the greater good.

We do have a Plan B in case the FBI gets lucky somehow and uncovers our plans. Starting this week, I'm spending full time at the warehouse with the assembly team. Should anything go wrong, we'll rush the assembly to completion, and I'll detonate the bomb immediately. It may not have quite the impact we hoped, but even a small nuclear explosion will ruin everyone's day.

> Where all my journeys end,
> If you can make a promise,
> If it's one that you can keep,
> I vow to come for you,
> If you wait for me,
> And say you'll hold,
> A place for me in your heart.
> — The Promise by Tracy Chapman

# 25
# THE PROMISE

Tonight, I brought April up to speed with events that happened after she left me in Miami. How Special Agent Toomey uncovered the secret backdoor in our hurricane model and threatened to put me in jail unless I cooperated in his counter-terrorism operation. How I moved to Chicago with Chewy in order to help more directly in the investigation. And finally, in direct violation of my security clearance, I told her the exact nature of that terrorism threat and the current status of our efforts to thwart it.

"Holy crap! I knew something was bothering you, but I had no idea it was anything like this."

"I think we're getting close to uncovering the key players in the attack, but I don't know if it will be in time to make any difference. Unless the other side makes a mistake."

"Have you seen any future headlines about the attack yet?"

"Not yet, so that means we should have at least another couple of weeks before the bomb explodes. Toomey thinks they're going to do it before the end of April."

"Do you think you'll be able to change the future if it looks like Chicago will get blown up?"

"I'm not sure but based on experience, the bigger and more devastating the future event, the less likely it is that I can change it. Best case, maybe I can shuffle the deck and make a less deadly alternative more probable."

"Is there anything else we can do?"

"That's why I'm telling you all this April. Aren't you supposed to be my spirit guide or something? I need some serious guiding here."

"I was sent here to guide you Jake, but only to help you use your abilities in the best way. I can't tell you how to prevent the apocalypse."

"Usually, you get some kind of premonition when I'm in danger. I was hoping you might have one of those. Last time your premonition gave us enough time to act and save the day."

"Sorry, I've got nothing. At least not so far. But you're right. If there is something in the future that puts you in danger, I would know about it in advance."

"I'm pretty damn sure that if that bomb explodes, both of us will be in danger – not to mention about 300,000 other people. Most likely I'll be canvassing the area where we suspect the bomb is being built when things go boom. So, danger is hardly the right word. Toast is the word I would use. *Burnt* toast."

"But isn't that good news? The deadly event is not showing up yet on either of our radar screens. So, either it never happens at all or it's farther out into the future."

"As soon as I see it, I'm getting you on a plane to someplace far away. You can stay at my place on the beach."

"I need to stay and help you Jake. It's what I do."

"No way. I can't lose you again. It's not going to happen."

"My gut says you're going to need me to stop this thing. I don't think you can do it on your own this time."

"Thanks for the vote of confidence. Either way, you can guide me by long distance phone call and text messages. No need for you to be in harm's way just because I must be."

"Don't you see Jake? For me to help you, I need to be close to you. That's the only way it works. That's why I was sent here."

"Then you'll be close to a dead man April. No way I survive this if that bomb explodes. My best chance is that you might see something in your premonition that could help us. You know like the location of the bomb or something."

"Usually, I get only enough information to save you Jake. It's probably not going to be enough to stop the bomb from exploding. My superiors tend to frown on that sort of thing. Too much interference."

"So how do you plan on saving me then?"

"By taking you with me to your beach house. You can pass along anything important to Agent Toomey by phone. Once the event shows up in your Mega Event Stream, we should leave. There's probably not much you can do by staying here anyway. The FBI is trained for this. You're not."

"It's my hometown April. I can't just leave. I need to do everything I can."

"Promise me, if you can't change the future and we don't come up with any information that might help, you'll leave with me before that bomb explodes."

"I guess."

"Promise me Jake."

"I promise."

"I hope this is not like the promise you once made to Jennifer. The one where you read her future after promising you wouldn't. Remember, that didn't turn out well for you, human."

"I'll try to keep that in mind."

Tempting Fate

I close my eyes.
Only for a moment and the moment's gone,
All my dreams,
Pass before my eyes, a curiosity.
Dust in the wind,
All they are is dust in the wind.
— Dust in the Wind by Kansas

# 26
# FUTURE SHOCK

Just as I'm beginning to feel hopeful that things may be alright after all, fate kicks me in the ass as usual. I'm sipping my morning latte, thinking about all the naughty things I can do with April after work, and then boom! Not boom in the sense of getting blown into radioactive dust. Boom in the sense that this morning's Mega Event Stream headline alerts me that twelve days from now, I will be blown into radioactive dust. On April fifteenth, the headline reads: **NUCLEAR BOMB BLAST ROCKS CHICAGO – THOUSANDS DEAD AND INJURED**. Details are sketchy as to the exact detonation location and cause but suffice to say that Tax Day in Chicago is going to be much worse than usual.

My first call is to April. I need to know if she knows anything else that may help.

"We're fucked. The bomb explodes in twelve days, on April fifteenth."
"How certain are you?"
"It's an 83% probability. That's about certain as my visions get."
"Sounds like one of those morally unambiguous situations. Are there any alternative outcomes you can select?"
"No. They're all grayed out. This is one of those freight train of fate things. The bomb will explode. Nothing can stop it. I did notice there was an unusual lack of detail in the Mega Event Stream. Nothing specific about the detonation location or the size of the explosion. I'm hoping you might have something more since I'm probably going to come out of this extra crispy."
"I started getting one my "DANGER! DANGER!" Jake Hedley warnings last night. I didn't get any details except you will be in the immediate blast range – somewhere in the near West Side."
"Anything else?"
"The warnings I get about danger to my Primaries are usually only detailed enough to get them out of harm's way. I did get something about "Premature Detonation." Does that mean anything to you?"

"Maybe. Let me check with Toomey and see if he can make anything of that."

So not much insight from April. My next call is to Agent Toomey.

"Bad news Nate. We only have twelve days. The bomb explodes on April fifteenth. Somewhere on the near West Side. Nothing specific on location or intensity. Thousands die."

"That's it? No details?"

"There is one thing – not sure what it means. Something about "Premature Detonation". That mean anything to you?"

"That could be a good thing. Nuclear bomb detonation requires very precise conditions for maximum effect. If something interrupts the arming process – say an FBI raid- it would force them to denotate prematurely. That could significantly limit the power of the explosion and minimize casualties."

"So, the best-case scenario is our team gets close enough to the bomb to rush things along and get vaporized in the process?"

"That sounds about right. No matter how badly they fuck up the detonation, everyone within several city blocks will be incinerated. Do you think we have any chance to stop the detonation entirely?"

"I'd say it's doubtful. My future visions come with an event probability. This one has an 83% chance of occurring. That bomb is going to blow, and I don't think there is anything likely to stop it. The only issue is how much we can rush them into exploding it before they're ready."

"Then that's what we'll do. I'll continue a full court press to find the bomb until twenty-four hours out. Then I'll pull out all resources except the immediate search team – volunteers only. The rest of the team will execute a cover story – probably a gas main leak – and evacuate as many people as possible in the likely target area."

"What can I do?"

"Assuming you're willing, continue your surveillance activities until the evacuation. Then I want you on a plane back to California. You're not to be anywhere near that explosion Jake."

"Honestly, I didn't know you cared."

"Orders from on high. You're too valuable an asset to risk on a likely suicide mission. Besides, we may have other plans for you. Don't forget I head up the Unexplained Phenomenon Investigation Service."

"How can I forget? U PIS me off all the time Toomey."

"Still with the acronym jokes? Really?"

"Sorry, can't help myself."

"Whatever Hedley. I'm going to have a car and a company jet standing by to get you out with the other evacuees. Either you come with us quietly or we'll drag you and your dog out in handcuffs – your choice. Doesn't matter to me."

The thought of Chewy being dragged out of town in handcuffs almost made me smile, but I managed to keep on topic. I needed Toomey to think I was fine with his plan.

"Don't worry Toomey. I'm no hero. I'll be long gone before that bomb explodes."

Now that I knew how to save Chicago, my fate was sealed.

Even before we knew the exact date of the bomb explosion, we had been surveilling the shit out of Harvey Slayton, aka, Kareem Musaffa, the Communications Lead for the Acquisitions Cell. Harvey couldn't take a piss without the HUMINT team knowing it – along with the quantity and color.

Unfortunately, Harvey almost never leaves his house, so I couldn't get a read on his future. Today, we decide to smoke him out using one of our smoking hot UPIS agents to knock on his door. She has some mail for him that was "mistakenly" delivered to her place down the street. Naturally, he opens the door to see what this lady wants. She flirts with him for a few moments and then hands him the letter. It's long enough for me to read his future from the van parked across the street. Nothing nefarious is going to happen to Harvey in the next twelve minutes, unless you count him spanking the monkey after his hot new neighbor departs. I'm sure the HUMINT team will determine the quantity and color of that too.

Now that I'm tuned into Harvey's "wavelength", I check his future every 30 minutes from the office. Finally, something interesting turns up. He's going to place a personal ad in the Chicago Tribute. It's a coded message to the Communications Team Lead of the Operations Cell – a person he does not know and has never met. Crap.

The ad reads as follows: For sale, Maytag Washer Model X3c700 (that's the message identifier). Recently serviced (latest acquisition request delivered successfully). Under 5 years old in good condition (cell has been compromised). Price $200 – Final offer (last communication – do not attempt future contact).

Toomey decides to send in the FBI SWAT Team to pick up Harvey at his house. His plan is to interrogate Harvey to see if he'll give up his personal ad codes. That way, we might be able to bring his Communications counterpart from the Operations Cell out into the open. It has low odds of success – these key cell members are high up in the terrorist hierarchy and are very dedicated. Usually, it takes weeks to break them without enhanced interrogation. We don't have weeks but it's our only lead and its worth a try.

Just before the SWAT Team arrives, I check Harvey's immediate future. Turns out he doesn't have one – now that his mission is complete, he must self-terminate. The next person to open his front door will join him in paradise. After a frantic call to Toomey, the SWAT Team is called off just in time. They watch as Harvey's house explodes into a fireball. I hope the virgins like their Jihadists on the crispy side.

> This is the day upon which we are reminded
> of what we are on the other three hundred and sixty-four.
> - Mark Twain referring to the first day of April

# 27
# APRIL'S FOOL

After another fruitless day of searching, Chewy and I are exhausted. Now that we have a fixed deadline to save the city, the pressure is enormous. April is coming by with dinner. She's been strangely silent since our call this morning, but I can't wait to see her. She's the only one who can ease my mind right now.

I'm expecting her to try to convince me to get out of Chicago sooner than Agent Toomey's deadline. After all, my Mega Event Stream visions are just probabilities of major events. Things could turn out differently (worse), and since my dying would hardly qualify as a major event, I might not see that coming.

As it turned out, I didn't see April's advice coming either.

"I think you may need to be there right before the bomb explodes."

"Say what now? As the possible new love of my life, I was hoping you might try to talk me out of doing that. Besides, what about that thing you made me promise?"

"You should really pay more attention to your promises Jake. What I said was, if you can't change the future and we don't come up with any information that might help, you'll leave with me before that bomb explodes. Turns out you *can* change the future, just by being there."

"And how exactly does that happen?"

"It's that premature detonation thing Jake. By being there, you force the terrorists to explode the bomb before they're ready. You're the Wild Card, remember? Your presence in this world changes it."

I had already come to the same conclusion after my talk with Toomey, but I needed to see how far April would go with this.

"If I find out where the bomb is, can't I just send in the cavalry? The FBI has highly trained people for this kind of thing."

"Maybe, but my sense is that you're the only possible variable here. It must be you who finds the bomb. I doubt there will be any time to call the cavalry."

"You're saying that the only way for me to save Chicago is for me to incinerate myself?"

"I won't allow that Jake. I'll be watching over you when the time comes. I can have you back at your apartment in a flash. It should be far enough away from the blast to be safe."

"I see what you did there. In a *flash*? Really?"

"You're not the only one who can make stupid puns."

"Let me get this straight. You want me to place myself – not to mention my dog – within spitting distance of a nuclear bomb about to go off. All to make the people setting off the bomb do it a bit earlier than they wanted. Is that about right?"

Chewy: Fuck that shit. This bitch is crazy.

"Why is Chewy snarling at me? What did he say?"

"Not important. How certain are you that you can get us out in time?"

"There's a good chance so long as you and Chewy stay close together. I can't transport anyone else though. I only have approval for the two of you."

"I'll have to keep the FBI team at a distance. Otherwise, they'll all be toast. Any idea how big the blast will be if I can get them to detonate prematurely?"

"No idea but I have a strong feeling that your intervention will make all the difference - if you can get there before the planned detonation time."

"That's pretty much what Toomey said. The key is to get them to set off the bomb before they complete the arming process. Or even better to prevent them from setting it off entirely, but as we know, that has low odds of happening."

"Are you guys any closer to finding the bomb location?"

"Not really. Our best lead from HUMINT turned out to be a dead end. Literally, he blew himself up before we could bring him in. Toomey still has Chewy and I doing a grid search of the general area, but we still have several square miles to cover with thousands of potential bomb locations. Chewy and I can only cover a few square miles a day – we'll need to get a lucky break."

"Is your search pattern just random within each grid?"

"Not exactly. The team identifies likely structures within each grid that would be suitable for bomb construction. Then we use an expanding square pattern to hit all those locations within the grid."

"Do you ever just use your intuition or your twelve-minute glimpses of the future to refine the search?"

"So far no. We've relied on the tried-and-true FBI search methods."

"Definition of insanity Doodle Boy. You have crazy amounts of intuition – it goes with your other abilities. I'd say use it. Follow the grid pattern but eliminate any targets that have a neutral feel. Focus only on those that feel suspicious to you. You'll save a bunch of time that way. Give yourself the best chance."

"Funny, Jennifer once told me to do something similar. To use my intuition more."

"How'd that work for you last time, Jake?"

Now we both know that Jennifer's intuition advice probably saved thousands of people from getting killed by hurricanes, but I wasn't going to just admit that. Her 11th dimensional head was already getting too big for my taste.

"Might be worth a try. But I can't speak for Chewy. I'm not sure he wants to risk getting his ass fried on a hunch. What do you say Chewy?"

Chewy: I believe I've already made myself crystal clear on the subject. I have other ways of expressing myself if my talking dog thing isn't working for you.

"I can tell he's not excited about it. Tell him if he does this, I may be able to get his balls back."

Chewy looks at April suspiciously and then looks at me.

Chewy: I don't trust her.

"Come on Chewy. You're the one who is always saying how good she smells and that I should listen to her. Time to follow your own advice."

Chewy: Easy for you to say, it's not your balls on the line.

"Can't lose what you don't have buddy. Take a chance."

Chewy: And you'd let me keep them this time?

"So long as you don't start humping small appliances again. Or my girlfriend."

Chewy: All right then. Deal. But if I get my ass blown off in this thing, I'm biting you on my way out.

"Chewy says he'd be happy to help."

"The devil is in the details" is an idiom that refers to a catch or mysterious element hidden in the details, meaning that something might seem simple at a first look but will take more time and effort to complete than expected and derives from the earlier phrase "God is in the details" expressing the idea that whatever one does should be done thoroughly, i.e., details are important.
 - Wikipedia

# 28
# THE DEVIL IS IN THE DETAILS

My team was not happy about moving up our Sword of Allah demonstration by two weeks. Not because we must now rush the bomb to completion during the most sensitive possible time. That, they were okay with. No, they were upset that we were all going to miss the Night of Destiny. The symbolism of destroying a major infidel city on the anniversary of Muhammed's enlightenment was just too good to give up. I finally had to tell them that the FBI is just too close to finding us. It's either detonate early or not at all. Each of us had already sacrificed too much to let it be in vain. Plus, the irony of destroying a major financial center on same day as the US income tax filing deadline has some appeal. Not exactly as meaningful as Muhammed's Night of Destiny, but since many people wait until the last day to file, the IRS is going to have a shit storm on their hands. Praise God.

I could care less about symbolism and calendar dates. For me as an engineer, the real issue is all the critical steps that must take place exactly as spec'd in order for the bomb to explode correctly. Those specifications are very sensitive and very precise. They can only be rushed so much. None of us have ever built anything that requires this level of precision. It won't be easy.

The bomb mechanism works like a gun – a rather fitting analogy, I think. The bomb casing is essentially a long tube. At one end is a shaped mass of uranium – just slightly below critical mass in size. At the other end of tube is another shaped mass of uranium, once again just below critical mass. Sitting behind that uranium is a propellent charge which will be used to shoot that hunk of uranium into the hunk at the other end of the tube. The uranium pieces must be shaped and milled with exact precision so that they fit together like a lock and key. The idea is to maximize the surface area of uranium that comes into contact for as long as possible.

The basic problem in making a fission bomb such as ours is getting a supercritical mass of material together fast enough so that the reaction does not blow the material apart before it can generate an appreciable explosive yield. Once the chain reaction begins it will almost immediately vaporize the uranium, thus stopping the reaction. The trick is to force that mass together long enough for a truly powerful chain reaction to occur. We only need a few millionths of a second worth of reaction and only a small fraction of the uranium will actually undergo fission. But in Einstein's world of nuclear physics, $E=MC^2$. That means even a tiny amount of mass (M) produces an enormous (speed of light squared times its mass) amount of energy (E). Twenty kilotons worth of TNT if we get it right. That should be enough to ruin everyone's day.

The idea behind our bomb is rather simple but the math and engineering behind it are not. The speed at which we smash the two masses of uranium together is critical. Too fast and we just blow the bomb apart before anything happens. Two slow and all we have is a rather large pipe bomb. The speed of the collision is impacted by many factors including the amount and type of propellent, the type of fuse being used, the amount and enrichment of uranium fuel, the materials used in the bomb itself, and even the environmental conditions when the bomb is detonated.

Of course, some of this was determined in advance based on the amount and type of uranium we had acquired. We spent months getting the right amount of propellant combined with the right fuse to set it off in a very precise manner. We spent many more months milling and shaping the uranium into the precise configuration necessary for maximum effect. All that work is almost done, and the bomb components are currently being (carefully) assembled. What remains now is to calibrate the fuse mechanism so that we get the precise amount of propellant explosive force we need to bring the uranium masses together in just the right way.

The fuse mechanism is basically a computer which needs to be programed with all kinds of parameters to precisely control the explosive force of the propellant. We use mathematical formulas to set those parameters based on the exact conditions – temperature, air pressure, humidity, etc. – under which the bomb will be detonated. This process takes time. We have a starting configuration almost ready which is based on our normal Chicago weather conditions this time of year. We'll need to adjust those settings for the exact conditions on our detonation day.

There is no doubt, God willing, that we can complete these tasks by our new deadline date. All the required materials for our Sword of Allah have now been acquired. The components are being assembled. It's tricky, painstaking work. Getting the shaped pieces of uranium in exactly the correct position within the gun tube is essential. The tolerances required are within a few thousandths of an inch. And uranium, while not extremely radioactive, is still very dangerous to handle. We have all been exposed to enough radiation that we'd probably die of cancer within a few years even if we were not killed in the explosion. As the saying goes when it comes to bacon and eggs, the chicken is involved but the pig is committed. We are the pigs.

Flight 93 was still in the air well after the three other planes had collided into the World Trade Center towers and the Pentagon, and the hijacked passengers were able to learn of those crashes over the course of the 37 calls they made from GTE air phones and cell phones. The happenstance created opportunities for heroism, which several passengers then amply supplied. Tom Burnett, 38, told his wife, "We're all going to die. There's three of us who are going to do something about it." Mark Bingham, 31, told the FBI, through his mother, that the hijackers claimed to have a bomb. The last words Jeremy Glick, 31, said to his spouse were, "We're going to rush the hijackers." But it was Todd Beamer, 32, connected with a GTE supervisor while attempting to reach his pregnant wife, who calmly and decisively uttered the iconic phrase: "Are you guys ready? Let's roll."
  - New York Magazine

# 29
# LET'S ROLL

Chewy and I are coming up empty on our daily searches. It's already April fourteenth. We've been out searching the grids every day for sixteen hours. I had to replace Chewy's biker boots twice already. We're both putting on a lot of miles. I bet Chewy will never complain about not getting out for walks enough again.

So far, we've met hundreds of people in the target area. It's not always a simple matter to vet them. Turns out that most people have layers – few are totally good or totally bad. Chewy can only give us a sense for just how good or how bad. Often, we have to get the HUMINT team to do background checks on the more ambiguous situations. That takes time and slows us down.

I've begun to take April's advice by using my intuition more – both to narrow the search pattern and to eliminate potential suspects. I'm worried we could be missing critical clues, but we are running out of time. There simply isn't time to investigate the semi-bad people we encounter; we have to focus on the ultra-bad. So now the wife beaters, the cheats, the thieves, the con men, and the violent gang members get a pass. We are after bigger prey.

Now Chewy and I can cover more ground in a day. Instead of just a square mile or two per day, we can almost do four. It's still not enough. We need some luck. Percolating in the back of everyone's mind is the real possibility that we may have already missed something in our previous searches. Maybe the terrorists didn't venture out that day. Maybe they did and we just missed them.

Toomey is going to pull us out of the field by sundown. The evacuation plan has already started. The news is reporting a major gas main leak. Everyone within ten miles of the target area will be evacuated. Only a small volunteer FBI team remains to scour the area. They will have almost no chance of success and will likely be killed unless Chewy and I find something soon.

The weight of our responsibility is overwhelming. Even Chewy feels it. Normally his doggy nature would require lifting his leg on every interesting vertical object we encounter. Now he marches along like a soldier, completely focused on the task. I'm proud of him. Whatever happens, Chewy has more than earned his SAC-D title as well as all our respect. Notwithstanding his service dog biker outfit. But hey, even heroes can be quirky right?

So, we solider on. Today our contacts have been rather sparse. It's a workday and this is an industrial area of town. Most people are inside working. People just venture out for smoking breaks and the food trucks. Chewy and I approach everyone we see. Our shtick has been well refined. Whenever we spot someone on the street (usually Chewy sees them first), Chewy strains at his leash pulling us towards the suspect as if the most interesting place in the world to pee was directly in their vicinity. Once we are within scent range, Chewy totally ignores the suspect and goes about his business. Within seconds, Chewy gives me his report. Most times, he just says "Pass" and we move on to the next person. For suspect buildings, we come inside the front door asking the first person we encounter whether this is the location for Windy City Auto Parts. Chewy gets a good sniff and sometimes a head scratch from the person. It's never Windy City Auto Parts, so we move on.

The next suspect building on today's search pattern is just ahead. It doesn't look like much. Just a small, dingy brick building with no sign out front. Our daily search brief identifies this building as being owned by a cosmetics company. The business license is for chemical processing. There is no one outside so we look for a door.

There is one small door in front and a loading dock in the alley. The windows are few and darkly shaded. For a rather old, almost decrepit structure, I notice an unusual number of security cameras. There are cameras at every corner, the front door, and several on the loading dock. There is some crime in this neighborhood, but it's not known as a high crime area. Plus, what can you steal from a chemical factory?

My intuition is pinging hard as we enter the front door. I feel the hairs on my neck standing up. Aside from the abundance of security cameras, there is nothing outwardly suspicious about this place, so I have no idea where this feeling is coming from. I guess that's why it's called intuition.

The first person we encounter is a man behind a desk. He looks like a security person and there are some TV monitors on his desk. A bit unusual for this area – I can't imagine they get many visitors – but still not all that out of the ordinary. We ask him about Windy City Auto Parts. He's very polite, saying "no" but that the name sounds familiar. He asks us to wait while he calls his supervisor whom he says, knows the area quite well.

While we wait, Chewy gives me the scoop on the security guy.

Chewy: This guy is dangerous. Be careful. He isn't necessarily a bad person, but he doesn't mind hurting someone to protect his colleagues. Not so different than some of your FBI buddies.

After a surprisingly brief few seconds, a second man comes out from behind an "Employees Only" door. He is tall, dark, and well dressed. Clearly a management guy.

"Hi. I'm Daryl. How can I help you?"
"Sorry, I'm afraid I'm a bit lost. We're looking for a place called Windy City Auto Parts. I don't have an address, but I was told it was somewhere around here."
"Need some parts for your biker dog's ride? (big smile)."
"For my wife's Volvo. It's a '94 wagon. Getting parts for that rust bucket is a bitch, but she loves the car for some reason. Heard that Windy City is the only place in town that might have what we need."
"They're just down the street. I've heard good things about them. Just head South three blocks and it's on your right."
"That's great. Thanks so much."
"Nice dog you have there. Is it a Golden Doodle?"
"Among a few other things, yes. He's a bit of a mutt."
"Well good luck on the Volvo parts."
"Thanks again."

And with that, Chewy and I are on our way. Chewy immediately confirms what I already suspect.

"You know these are the guys, right?"
"I got a really bad vibe from them – particularly from Daryl."
"He's off the charts bad, Jake. The worst kind of bad. The kind that thinks he's good."
"As we turned to leave, I read Daryl's future."
"And?"
"You're not going to like it. He doesn't have one and neither do we."
"Let's just call in the FBI team and get the hell out of here then. We've played our part. We found the bomb."
"There's no time. Daryl made us; he knows we're Feds. He's going to detonate the bomb in ten minutes. If I call in the team, they'll just get blown up on the way over."
"What do we do?"

"There is no way we can stop the bomb from detonating. But maybe we can make the explosion smaller by rushing him. He needs the full ten minutes to set the fuse. We can't let him have that time."

"I don't know about you, but I don't have a vest and an assault rifle under my outfit. How the hell do we get back in there?"

"When I read his future, I looked at the alternative possible outcomes. There are no possible outcomes that prevent the explosion, but there is one where we storm the building and force him to detonate early. I don't know if that will be enough to reduce the force of the explosion, but I think we have to try."

"So that's it then. We're toast?"

"Even if we ran, we couldn't get away fast enough. What do you say Chewy? Shall we be heroes?"

"I'd rather get my balls cut off again. But if we're going to die anyway - what the hell."

"Good because I've already selected that outcome. Let's roll."

Crunch Time: a critical moment or period (as near the end of a game) when decisive action is needed.
- MERRIAM-WEBSTER UNABRIDGED

# 30
# CRUNCH TIME

I watch as the man and his biker dog head out the door and down the street. There is no sign of any police presence outside. No white panel vans. No black Suburban's. No snipers on the rooftops. No drones buzzing around. Nothing. All good in the hood.

And who ever heard of a Federal officer patrolling with a Golden Doodle in a biker outfit? Ridiculous. Paranoid. But somehow, I know.

I figure we might have ten minutes before a Fed SWAT team starts busting in the doors. We must be ready. Now.

Our detonation team is already here working on the final preparations. Everything is almost set for tomorrow's demonstration. They are making a few final microscopic adjustments to the uranium fuel positions and starting the programming of the fuse for tomorrow's forecasted weather conditions.

No time for finesse now. We'd have to go with what we've got. I run down to the main assembly room screaming for the team's attention.

"WE HAVE TO DETONATE! THE FBI IS ON THEIR WAY! GET EVERYTHING READY FOR IMMEDIATE DETONATION!"

I pull the head of the detonation team aside while everyone is scurrying to close the bomb casing and start the detonation sequence.

"How much time do you need for maximum effect?"

"We need ten to fifteen minutes to finish up and close the bomb casing. We didn't finish fine tuning the fuel positions, but it should be close enough, God Willing."

"Make it happen in ten. Can you rig a Deadman Switch for me to detonate immediately in case we can't finish in time?"

"Already done sir. I'm plugging it in for you now."

A Deadman Switch is a fail-safe mechanism for the suicide bomber. Normally your typical suicide bomber wants to delay detonation until the best possible moment when the most people, or at least the targets of the attack, are in range. The switch acts like a normal detonation button except in reverse. Instead of pressing the button to detonate, you just release it. That way, if the godless infidels get lucky and a sniper shoots off the top of your head, you don't have to press the button, you just let go - which of course is the inevitable reaction when sudden death occurs. And boom, your friendly neighborhood suicide bomber is in paradise with all those virgins or whatever having achieved martyr status by blowing up everyone nearby. And hey, he was already dead from the bullet anyway, so everybody wins.

I hope I'm wrong about the man and his dog, but its best to be prepared as my mama always told me. Worse case, we'll have gone through an unplanned dry run for the Sword of Allah. Practice makes perfect. Another time-honored expression from my parents.

As the team frantically prepares the bomb, I make final preparations myself. I pray to God that his Will is smiling upon me now as I get ready to meet my destiny. I am at peace knowing that I've done everything I could to make this world a better place during my short time here. I'll miss my earthly life, but I know there will be better things ahead.

I smile as I contemplate my new home in paradise with all those servants and all those maidens with their dark eyes. Maybe God will even throw in a few blue-eyed blondes if all goes well.

That's when I hear the shots ring out. The first thing I see as I open my eyes is a rather angry looking Golden Doodle running towards me. An image of Achmed the Dead Terrorist flashes in my mind. Premature Detonation doesn't seem all that funny at the moment. Don't laugh. I KILL YOU!

**Dr. Strangelove**: Of course, the whole point of a Doomsday Machine is lost, if you keep it a secret! Why didn't you tell the world, EH?
**Ambassador de Sadesky**: It was to be announced at the Party Congress on Monday. As you know, the Premier loves surprises.
- Dr. Strangelove or: How I Learned to Stop Worrying and Love the Bomb

# 31
# DOOMSDAY

Suddenly, both Chewy and I are inside the dingy brick cosmetics laboratory. As always, when I select an alternative outcome during my twelve-minute glimpse of the future, whatever needs to happen to cause that outcome, just happens. Apparently, we entered through a previously unseen side door. Now we are standing in a large room that resembles a factory floor. Directly in front of us facing away, stands an armed security guard holding an automatic weapon. Farther inside the room, there are about ten people all standing around a large cylindrical object. They are dressed in white lab coats, but I suspect they are not engaged in creating a new line of mascara.

Under ordinary conditions, I would have no chance to overpower an obviously well-trained guard holding an assault rifle – armed only with a rather irritated Golden Doodle. But anyone paying attention knows by now that I rarely deal with ordinary conditions. I tend to tempt fate just a bit by changing things into the non-ordinary. I read the guard's immediate future and see he's about to turn around and shoot me. In the twitch of an eye, I look for a better outcome. Here's one: "JAKE KICKS GUARD IN BALLS FROM BEHIND." That understandably makes him loose his grip on his AK47 and I grab it. Then I shoot him.

Now to be honest, I have no idea what kind of weapon the guy is carrying. It's just that every terrorist movie I've ever seen shows the bad guys with AK47's. So, I'm going with that. All I know is that it has a trigger and the bullets come out the front.

So, I pick that outcome, and everything goes according to plan until I press the trigger. Apparently even AK47s have safeties so the terrorists don't kill themselves by mistake. The guard begins to recover from his testicle assault and heads toward me with bad intent. I desperately start flipping switches and moving stuff around on the riffle. Fortunately, I hit the safety switch before the magazine release lever and one round out of about hundred hits the guard. The rest spray across the room in the general direction of the bomb and the white coats. The guard is still moving toward me until he realizes that about half his neck is missing and his rather large head is tilting badly to one side. Just like Wiley Coyote in the Road

Runner cartoon, once he notices the problem, the guard drops like a rock. Beep! Beep!

But now the lab guys in the white coats are shooting back at me. My first thought is, since when do lab workers have guns? Come on now, who comes up with this shit? I mean the worst I was expecting was maybe they'd start chucking lab beakers at me or something. But noooooo, these guys were firing actual bullets. None of the rounds got anywhere near me, of course, proving once again that it's stupid to give lab guys guns. I press the trigger again, pointing my AK47 or whatever in their general direction. The bullets miss everything but make so much noise that the lab guys scatter into the shadows. All except one guy wearing a suit. Daryl.

Before I can fire again, I see Chewy making a mad rush directly towards Daryl and the bomb. I can't shoot without hitting Chewy, so I do the only thing I can think of. I run after my dog. Towards the guy about to set off the nuclear bomb.

I see Daryl reach towards the bomb and grab something. At that moment, Chewy launches himself towards Daryl's balls with teeth flashing. He misses his target by just an inch or two but gets a good piece of Daryl's thigh muscle. Daryl howls in pain and flails his damaged leg trying to get Chewy to let go. Just as I get close, Daryl manages to free himself with a violent kick that sends Chewy flying through the air behind me.

I point my rifle at Daryl's head. He's bleeding like a stuck pig – a fitting analogy I think – but still manages to smile.

"So what, it's not enough to blow up my hometown. Now you have to kick my dog?"

"To be fair he was trying to rip my balls off, but I am sorry. Normally dogs like me."

"Chewy is an unusually good judge of character. He says you smell bad."

"Since when does the FBI use hyper-intuitive, killer Golden Doodles to assist their agents?"

"It's a rather new unit in the FBI. We're called UPIS. That was Special Agent Chewy you just punted. He's going to be really pissed at you."

"Makes sense given his unit name."

"Don't get me started on the name thing. But if you move toward that bomb, I'm going to use more traditional FBI tactics to shoot you in the head."

"It won't matter. I've already got the Deadman's Switch."

I don't know what that means, so I quickly check my future for a clue. Oh shit. Not good.

There are not a lot of good choices left. The white coats are beginning to emerge from the shadows, guns raised. If I give them time, they will finish the arming process. If I shoot Daryl, the Deadman's Switch will immediately detonate the bomb.

I look back towards Chewy and see him limping towards me.

"What do you think SAC-D? Shall we go out in a blaze of glory?"

Chewy: Can I bite him again first?

Daryl of course cannot hear Chewy's reply and responds only to my question.

"Only God can save you now and I think he's on my side."
"Well one thing's for sure, he's definitely not a Bears fan."
"I know. When the hell are they going to get a decent quarterback?"
"At the moment it looks like never."

With that, I shoot the remaining twenty rounds into Daryl's head. Nobody insults my Bears.

I never even see the flash.

At the outset of our work, we said we were looking backward in order to look forward. We hope that the terrible losses chronicled in this report can create something positive – an America that is safer, stronger, and wiser. That September day, we came together as a nation. The test before us is to sustain that unity of purpose and meet the challenges now confronting us.
- The 9/11 Commission Report

## 32
## AFTERMATH

In the days and months that follow the first nuclear terror attack on US soil, much was written about the explosion and the events that led up to it. There is no mention of anyone named Jake Hedley or his dog Chewy. Just as there was no mention of the hundreds of other unidentified people who were instantly incinerated in the explosion. Thousands more were injured by the blast and the sudden release of radiation.

All that is publicly known is that a secret FBI team had been investigating the terrorist cell for months and saved hundreds of thousands of innocent people from certain death. This secret team discovered the bomb location just hours before it was scheduled to be detonated – ultimately forcing the terrorists to explode their bomb before it was ready.

The bomb contained nearly three hundred pounds of partially enriched uranium. If properly detonated, it would have the explosive power of about twenty kilotons of TNT - just a bit larger than the bomb that destroyed Hiroshima. It would have obliterated almost everything within a six square mile area from Cicero to Soldiers Field. Over a million people live and work in that general vicinity. Scientists estimate that at least one hundred thousand of them would have died – probably more like two hundred thousand if you counted those that would die withing six months from bomb related injuries.

Instead, the bomb only achieved a blast amounting to a fraction of that - about one hundredth of a kiloton of TNT. It was enough to destroy about five city blocks with significant blast and radiation impacts extending out to about twice that distance. Total casualties may never be fully known, but at least 650 people died immediately from the explosion and another 2,300 sustained significant injury. All told, the second most costly terrorist attack in the US after 9/11.

But the city will recover. The bomb damage is already being cleared away to be stored in underground radiation-proof storage areas. Ground zero of the explosion will need to remain uninhabited for several generations, but that only encompasses about one square mile. Outside that area, the radiation is low enough to be cleared away along with the rubble and about one foot of topsoil.

The reasons for the partial detonation may never be fully known, but we do know that the terrorists were unable to complete the delicate arming process before the FBI closed in. It is likely they did not have time to fully program the bomb fuse before detonation. The day the bomb exploded was about ten degrees colder than normal which would impact the fuse settings. Most likely, the bomb propellant that sent the two pieces of Uranium crashing into each other was not set to explode with enough force. The impact speed of the uranium collision was probably insufficient to attain critical mass for a long enough time. Only a tiny fraction of the uranium underwent nuclear fission before being vaporized. But that small ball of uranium briefly reached temperatures and pressures greater than those at the center of the sun. Fortunately for the City of Chicago, it was a very small ball.

As for the terrorists, we believe everyone immediately involved was killed in the explosion. Their names and nationalities are just now being released. Planning and financing of the attack originated from an Al Qaeda cell in Syria. The attack had been planned over several decades during which time they established deep cover sleeper cells in Chicago and acquired hundreds of pounds of partially enriched uranium.

Within one month of the explosion, US intelligence identified the Syrian Al Qaeda cell that planned and financed the attack. A few weeks later, a Navy Seal Team assaulted the terrorist compound in Syria, capturing or killing everyone inside. They found the names of many other Al Qaeda members who helped acquire the uranium fuel and other bomb components for the attack on encrypted computer files within the compound. All these operatives were eventually killed by US drone strikes within their home countries.

Paradise must be running out of virgins.

*Just when you thought it was safe to be dead.*
*- Return of the Living Dead Part 2*

# 33
# THE LIVING DEAD

The last thing I remember is waiting for a flash. Then nothing. Now here I am lying on my couch. April is standing nearby with a concerned look.

No wonder she's concerned, I must look like toasted shit. Because that's how I feel. Every inch of me hurts. My skin feels like it has been peeled off. Every place where my body touches the couch feels like a needle poking me. I can't move and I think my ears are bleeding.

"So, is this your idea of a rescue?"

"We had a bit of a timing problem, I'm afraid."

"You call this a timing problem? A timing problem is like when your carburetor needs adjusting. I feel like my face is melting."

"You do look like hell to be honest."

"What the hell happened?"

"Okay, first the good news. You and Chewy saved Chicago. Well, most of it anyway."

"Did the bomb go off?"

"Yeah, that's the not so good news. It exploded but not all the way. You forced them to explode the bomb before they were ready. The fuse-thingy wasn't set properly so only a little piece of the bomb exploded. They're saying about 10 city blocks were partially destroyed."

"How many people died?"

"Too early to say, but they estimated more than 500 people died immediately in the blast."

"Fuck. You call that Not So Good News? I can't wait to hear the bad news."

"Jake, if you hadn't forced them to prematurely detonate, hundreds of thousands would have been killed."

"What's the bad news then?"

"I tried to get you and Chewy out of there before the detonation. I was late by about three hundredths of a second."

"That doesn't sound too bad. Not much happens in so short a time."

"Gamma radiation is the first emission from a fission reaction. Gamma rays travel at the speed of light. Do the math."

"So basically, I just have a bad sunburn, right?"

"If by bad you mean standing naked in front of a death ray then yes, a very bad sunburn. Gamma rays are the most energetic and dangerous of all electromagnetic radiation. We use them to kill cancer cells."

"That does sound bad. So why exactly did you let me get shot by this death ray darling?"

"The timing surprised me. I didn't expect you to shoot Daryl when you did."

"Well, he was holding the trigger to a nuclear bomb and his ten heavily armed lab assistants were about to shoot me. Seems like some of that might have given you a clue."

"You were talking to him about football for heaven's sake! Who shoots someone in the head while talking sports?!"

"He was talking shit about the Bears. He deserved it."

"Next time a bit of a heads up would be nice."

"Am I going to die or what?"

"You absorbed too much radiation Jake. Your body won't survive this."

"I guess I knew that the moment I woke up here with a melty face. I was just hoping you might have some way to save me. You know, being an Angel and all."

"Don't be so dramatic. You are made of energy Jake. A big annoying mass of energy. You, me, Chewy, and everybody else. Energy cannot be created or destroyed – only transformed. You'll be fine."

"How will I be fine without my body?"

"It was pretty cute, but you'll get a new one. I'll pick it out."

"Will I still be me?"

"Sure. We'll need to reboot you, but since you saved Chicago and everything, you get to keep all your memories."

"What about Chewy?"

"He's toast. But not to worry. Just like you, his energy survives. You'll see him again."

"Will I see you again?"

"Is that what you want?"

"I want that most of all."

"We can arrange that. After all, you'll still need supervision."

"Will I be like you?"

"You wish. You won't be an 11th dimensional entity like me – you're not nearly evolved enough for that. You'll just be the same, not quite normal 3-D guy you were before."

"What about you? Will you be the same? Will you remember me this time?"

"I will remember you Jake, but I'm thinking of changing things up a bit. I know you prefer blondes. I was thinking I'd be Jennifer again. Does that work for you?"

"I can live with that."

"Yes, I think you will."

*Don't go changing,*
*To try and please me,*
*You never let me down before,*
*Don't imagine you're too familiar,*
*And I don't see you anymore...*
*- Just the Way You Are by Billy Joel*

# 34
# A FEW MODIFICATIONS

They say you can't go home again. But I did. In almost every way possible. Most of all, I have Jennifer back. She is my home now, wherever we live.

According to official FBI records, UPIS consultant and HUMINT specialist, Jake Hedley, was back in FBI headquarters downtown when the blast occurred. He had been ordered to stand down as the anticipated detonation time approached. He is credited with helping the team uncover the terrorist plot and pin down the bomb location. Just one more member of the crack team that saved the city from almost certain destruction.

Unofficially, Special Agent Toomey knows I was a bit more involved than that. His investigation revealed that the terrorists somehow became aware that the FBI was about to close in, and he suspects I had a hand in making them detonate the bomb before they were ready.

I can understand his suspicion. For one thing, Chewy and I dropped out of sight for about a week after the blast. Then I mysteriously reappeared back at the beach in California, reporting back in by phone as if nothing had happened. I congratulated him and his team on a job well done. I know he believes that I somehow forced the premature detonation, but he has no explanation for how I could have survived.

To his credit, Toomey managed to hide his suspicions and wished me well. He even asked about Chewy. Later when I went to reapply for my old job at the National Hurricane Center, he gave me a glowing recommendation. I guess it takes a certain ability to accept the seemingly impossible if you're going to head up a team that specializes in the paranormal.

Toomey did ask me one favor in return for his cover story. He asked if I'd be willing to help his team in the future, should the need arise. I readily agreed. Saving people from disasters, natural and otherwise, seems to be my calling. I might as well accept it.

Now I'm back in Miami with Jennifer and Chewy. The National Hurricane Center hired me back in my old job as a hurricane forecasting analyst. I took a significant salary cut from before, but it feels good to be back doing something I'm good at. Especially something that won't likely involve getting blasted by lethal gamma radiation.

Jennifer moved back in with me. We rented a house near our old neighborhood. In many ways, we picked right up where we left off. Except now there are no secrets between us. We share everything together. Almost.

"I see Chewy got his balls back."
"Yeah, he insisted. I told him if he starts humping my leg again, it's back to the vet."

Chewy: Tell her not to worry. I've evolved quite a bit since those days. Hey, whatever happened to that vacuum cleaner we used to have?

"I'm sure Chewy appreciates your efforts."
"And how about the new me? I had to work from your old pictures. Did I get everything right?"
"Perfect. If anything, you're even hotter than Jennifer 1.0. You fill out that new bra quite nicely."
"I figured you wouldn't mind a slight enhancement."
"Good call. I can't keep my eyes, hands, and other parts off of them."
"I see you haven't evolved that much from Jake 1.0. Not that I mind a little caveman now and then."
"Any other enhancements I should know about?"
"Find out for yourself. A woman doesn't share all her secrets. What about you? Are you happy with the new body I picked out for you?"
"It looks just like my old one. I thought you'd make me look different."
"I'm rather fond of the old one. Besides, no one alive saw you die in the blast, so I figured it'd be simpler just to keep the same ole Jake. Less muss and fuss."
"I notice you *did* make a few modifications. There's a certain part of me that is no longer just on the "high side of average" – size wise."
"Hey, I got to pick out the new you, so I made a few changes just for me. Nobody else will notice. At least no one *better* notice."
"Don't worry Jennifer. I've learned it's a bad idea to piss off an Angel."
"See, you're evolving already."


## THE END


Continue reading the first chapter of the next book in the Fate Series, **Trusting Fate.**

And then one day you find ten years have got behind you.
No one told you when to run, you missed the starting gun.
— Time, Roger Waters

# 1
# TIME CHANGE

Sometimes no matter how hard you try, or how often, you just can't seem to get things right. I should know - do-overs are my thing. I bet most of you can think of a few times in your life that you'd love to relive again. Maybe it was that perfect day. One that you think about whenever you are down, and it puts a smile on your face. Maybe it was a time when you had a decision to make, and you choose the wrong path. That one time where you zigged when you should have zagged. The girl that got away because you didn't take your shot when you had the chance. That promotion you lost because you didn't read the politics correctly. The words you said in anger to someone you loved that can't be taken back. If you just had another shot, maybe you could put things right. Do things differently. Or maybe just have that great feeling again.

My name is Jacob Pilgrim. There have been many moments in my past that I'd like to do over again. Sometimes to correct a mistake and put things right. Sometimes just because I cherish the memory so much that I want to relive that moment again. The thing that makes these experiences different for me is that I actually *can* go back and relive or redo them. And I often do.

I was born with an ability to affect time. To slow it down. To rewind the past few minutes. And eventually, to redo any event in my past. It started when I was a child. My mom married this new guy after my father died. To a seven-year-old boy, he seemed huge and scary. At first, he was all nice and friendly, but eventually he became angry and violent. He would slap my mom and sometimes hurt me too. I became very good at predicting his moods and trying to stay out of his way when I sensed danger. My mom was not very good at that. She would provoke him at all the wrong times. Looking back, I wonder if maybe this was intentional. Not because she wanted to be hurt, but because she wanted his attention. Even negative attention to her was better than no attention.

When my new dad would come home, I'd immediately read his mood. It was easy, almost like he was wearing a hat with a flashing red warning light – STAY BACK FIFTY FEET OR I'LL POUND THE CRAP OUT OF YOU. I was always amazed that my mom couldn't read the sign or even see the warning light. I'd watch to see what happened from a distance. It was like watching a train speeding toward a broken section of track. You knew it was going happen, but you didn't know exactly how or when. In my mind, events seemed to slow down so I could easily see just how that train was going to wreck. And like any good train wreck, you just can't look away when you know it's going to happen. No matter how much you might want to.

Mom: Why do you always have to come home so late? Dinner is cold.

The scariest thing about my new dad was how normal he could be right before he was about to blow. His speech would slow. He would lower his voice. Every word was carefully enunciated. His tone was eerily calm. To me, it sounded like the rattle of a snake's tail.

Dad: Tough day at work. Sometimes I feel like I work with a bunch of morons. What's for dinner?

Mom: Cold spaghetti and meatballs. Thanks to you.

That huge hand would come out of nowhere. SLAP! The sound would be sharp and piercing. It hurt my ears. Not as much as it hurt my mom though.

This little scenario would happen repeatedly, in one form or another, every few weeks. It scared me so much that I would fantasize ways that I might stop it from happening. I'd imagine that I could just slow everything down. Maybe give me time to do something. Warn my mom. Diffuse the situation somehow. I just needed more time to think of what to do. I was never very fast on my feet when it comes to thinking of the right thing to do or say.

I learned to slow things down in my mind. We can all do this. Think what happens when you experience something terrifying in your life. The split seconds before that car slams into yours when they run a red light. Your senses are heightened. You can feel your body tense. Every aspect of the scene unfolding is observed in great detail. The motion of the converging cars slows down. You see every glint of light reflecting off the paint. The expressions on the faces of the other driver and passengers. An incredible stream of thought races through your head faster than time would ever allow. Your mind calculates the trajectories and impact points. You see clearly that there is no way to avoid the collision – only reduce the impact. Instinctively, you take evasive action – almost like you and your car are connected telepathically. All the while random thoughts race through your head. Where did that car come from? I didn't see him until it was too late. Is my seatbelt fastened? You imagine the impact before it happens. What it will feel like. How it will sound. All this in the fraction of a second before the vehicles collide.

I would do all this each time my new dad was about to blow. I'd slow down the action. Whereas before my dad's hand seemed to come from nowhere, now I could see him winding up for the strike. I could see his facial expression change from a serene calm to a crazed rage. I could see exactly where that hand was going to strike my mom. Usually, it was her face but sometimes it would be her arm or her chest. In the beginning, that was all I could do. I could slow everything down to see exactly what happened and what was going to happen.

Eventually, I learned to do more. I would slow down time further and further. In my head, I would shout "STOP!" and the scene would slow to a crawl. All this accomplished at first was to give the terrified observer (me) more time to appreciate every aspect of the event. But then something odd happened. Instead of just being frozen in time along with the rest of the events unfolding around me, I could think. And I could move. I could act in normal time when everyone else was moving in extreme slow motion. At first, all I would do is run away so I wouldn't hear that piercing sound of the slap. Then I began to wonder if I could do more. The next time I decided to scream "NO!" as loud as I could before that hand even began its wind up. That worked the first few times. My dad was so shocked by my sudden shout that it derailed his crazy train before the track ran out. My clueless mom would look at me like I was nuts and my dad would just jerk his head like he was shaken out of a trance. Which I guess in a way was exactly what happened. Once his train derailed, he would just walk away with a confused look on his face and the situation was diffused.

Nothing works forever though. People adapt. Fate continues on its track. My dad learned to anticipate my outbursts and would steel himself in advance. The hand would continue its windup unfettered by any extraneous noise from me. I learned to adapt as well.

I tried moving objects around when I slowed time. Turns out I could do whatever I wanted. The next time it happened, I picked up the nearest heavy object that my seven-year-old body could swing. That turned out to be my mom's rolling pin. I hit my dad just below the knee as his big hand began its windup. I had time to return both the rolling pin and myself to our original positions. My dad never knew what happened. One moment he was experiencing his usual sudden rage. The next he was on the floor howling in pain with a broken knee. During his several days in the hospital and several more weeks of recovery, all was quiet at home. My dad never figured out what happened, and the doctors could offer no explanation. It was like an act of God. Maybe it was.

Ever since the "accident," my dad treated us differently. I think he became afraid of his temper. He didn't hit me or my mom anymore. Whenever his rage began to build and his warning light began flashing, he would immediately leave the room and go off by himself. As he walked out of the room, he would also glance my way. I think he knew it was me but didn't want to test his theory. Whatever, life got better.

David F. Paulsen

Over the years, my ability to slow time served me well. As long as I could anticipate something bad happening, I could usually prevent it. But not all bad things can be predicted in advance. Sometimes fate catches you by surprise. That traffic accident. That time when the ladder slips while you're cleaning out the gutter. All those times when someone catches you doing something you shouldn't. In these cases, I could still slow down time but never stop it entirely. Once the bad thing happened, the consequences would invariably occur, no matter how much I slowed things down. Until one day.

It was my freshman year in college. Unlike most freshmen who plow through their first year at the low end of the social totem pole – somewhere between algae and pond scum in the eyes of most of our female classmates – I had a car and therefore was somewhat more socially acceptable. I actually had a girlfriend – a frosh but she was a girl and she rather liked me. We had dated a few months and I really liked her. But I was an eighteen-year-old male, so I pretty much liked all women. Hell, I could get hard looking at linoleum. That led to the classic dilemma for all young males. Invariably when you are with one girl, other girls become more interested in you. It's like you've been prequalified as a potential mate. This was all new to me. I wasn't used to having a steady girlfriend and had never considered myself particularly attractive to the female population. When another of my classmates- a very hot, sexy one - started to flirt with me, I was immediately captivated. Any potential hesitations I may have had about cheating on my girlfriend, dropped like a pine tree cut down by a chain saw. Soon we were banging up a storm in my dorm room. If it had ended there, things might have been fine. Of course, having just one bite of the apple is never enough. We began to meet up between classes – sometimes at my dorm and sometimes at hers. She was more addictive than chocolate. I'd even think of her while I was having sex with my girlfriend. That made me excited and guilty at the same time. Eventually, the inevitable happened. We got caught. My girlfriend walked in on us. I tried to stop time, but it was too late, she'd already seen us. All I could do was watch in slow motion as her facial expression changed from happy and excited to one of hurt and sadness. Regret slammed into me like a hammer. My girlfriend and I were not in love, but we were very close and the last thing on earth I wanted to do was hurt her. But I had hurt her and now I was forced to experience every single moment of her pain in extreme detail. I didn't want to return to normal time and face the consequences. I kept picturing in my mind how I could have prevented this if only I had known. If I could just rewind the clock a few minutes, I could fix this. I pictured myself ten minutes earlier, just as my new hot friend was walking up to my room. I saw my bed, freshly made, not yet rumpled. The door was still closed. I was alone. I desperately wanted to return to that moment. In my mind, I screamed out a single word. "REWIND!" Suddenly I was back there. I looked at my watch. It was ten minutes earlier, before any of my female visitors had arrived. I knew what I had to do. It was simple. I just needed to leave. Get out of Dodge. Step out the back, Jack. Make a new plan, Stan. I ran out the door before anyone saw me. I kept running until I was safely out of sight.

Later both girls called me. First the hot new one. She was upset that I had stood her up. She started to yell at me. I calmly informed her that I was dating someone else and had decided to be a good boy for a change. Her response was interesting. She hung up in anger as I expected. But then, almost immediately, called me back to see if she could change my mind. She couldn't. Next my girlfriend called. She was disappointed that she tried to surprise me, and I wasn't home. I told her she should try again, and I'd have a surprise for *her*. It was the first time in my life I bought a girl flowers for no occasion. I just wanted to see her smile and erase the memory of her pain that never happened.

I learned several important lessons that day. If you cheat, you'll eventually get caught. If you care about someone, be careful not to hurt them. And most importantly, if you do fuck up and something bad happens, rewind ten minutes and do the right thing.

Life has moved on since then, but that experience changed me in a fundamental way. Long after my freshman girlfriend and I broke up and we moved on with our lives, I continued using my control over time to get out of trouble. I'd either slow time to prevent trouble or rewind time to fix whatever trouble I caused. After years of doing this, my attitude towards life began to change. I became bolder. Less cautious in my actions. I didn't fear consequences because there never were any. I could prevent the consequences from happening, no matter how many stupid things I did. Bar fights? Why take any shit from drunk Neanderthals when I could land as many punches as I wanted before they could complete their first swing? Why not test out my new Corvette's top speed on that deserted straightaway? Speeding tickets? No problem. Rewind ten minutes and slow down before the speed trap. Maybe you think that girl you just met might be down to fuck, but you don't want to spoil things by being too aggressive. Why not try anyway? If she gets mad, just rewind and take it slower. My ability to affect time gave me tremendous freedom, but it also turned me into more of a jerk. I wasn't as nice as I used to be. Life without consequences changed me into someone that I probably would not want as a friend.

There are only two things that I worry about. First is death. If I do something that results in my sudden, unexpected death, I'm pretty sure there'd be no rewinding from that. Dead is dead. The second is delayed consequences from prior bad decisions. Turns out there are moments in life when you make a decision or do something where the consequences are not immediately apparent or are more long term in nature. Rewinding ten minutes in those cases does not help. Once that initial act is done, your path is chosen, and your fate is sealed. Most of the key milestones in life are like that. Career decisions. Marriage. Having children. Not having that lab test your doctor recommended. Things like that. In those situations, I am just as clueless as anyone else. Maybe that's why I have so much difficulty making those big decisions in life. Unlike my normal day-to-day actions, these big decisions have consequences that I cannot anticipate or avoid. Let me give you one example that haunts me still.

Several years ago, I lived in Reston, VA and I was struggling with one of life's less pleasant situations. One that most of us experience at one time or another. The longest romantic relationship of my life was ending. Even though I knew it was for the best because whatever love there had been between us was long gone, it was hard. Sometimes people in your life can be like an addiction. You know they aren't good for you, but it's hard to imagine life without them. That's how it was. In the midst of extricating myself from my former love, I met someone.

At the time, she seemed like just the lifeline I needed to move forward, past the pain of separation. Her name was Katrina. She was a free spirit, wild, carefree, and unaffected. She loved people and she loved life. Quite different than the woman I was leaving or anyone I had met before.

Katrina had been my dental hygienist for years. We had always been friendly, but over the past few months, I'd been seeing the dentist more often. Everything from cracked filings, to broken crowns, to root canals. That was about the same time as my relationship started going off the tracks. One day after a particularly lengthy root canal procedure, she took me aside to give me instructions on pain management. Most of those instructions had to do with being sure to take my pain meds BEFORE the Novocain wears off. I was her last appointment of the day, so I walked her to her car. On impulse I invited her for coffee after my follow-up appointment scheduled for the next Saturday. Saturdays are only half days in her dental office so I figured she might be free. And she was.

Over coffee, I learned several things about my pretty dental hygienist. First thing I noticed was her easy rapport with people. I knew she was outgoing and friendly, but since we'd never had a real conversation – at least not a two sided one since my mouth was usually numb and full of cotton – I didn't realize just how much fun she could be. I told her that I'd just gotten out of a long-term relationship and how difficult that was. She empathized and told me stories of her own past relationships – both with men and women. Katrina confided she was bi-sexual which added an interesting and unexpected twist to our conversation. Fortunately for me, she was currently in her "men" phase.

That initial coffee date led to several more encounters. Katrina and I became good friends. She helped me see the possibilities in life and how much fun life could be with just the right person. There was a definite sexual attraction between us, but being fresh out of my relationship, I wasn't ready to jump right into a new one. Katrina somehow knew that and maintained a certain distance. That distance didn't prevent her from teasing the shit out of me though – letting me know just how much fun she could be if only circumstances were different.

She shocked me once when we went out to dinner. I had picked her up and we spent a few moments kissing in my car before we left. Kissing was as natural as breathing to Katrina, so it seemed like no big deal – just a bit of affection between friends. Or so I thought. Dinner was on the second floor and we took the elevator up. I pushed the button and the doors closed. At that moment, Katrina pushed the stop button and suddenly pinned me against the elevator wall, kissing me hard while roughly grabbing my cock. After a few seconds, she just let go, released the stop button, and continued on as if nothing had happened. After recovering from the initial shock, I gave her my patented "what the fuck?" look which she returned with an evil smile. Neither of us mentioned it again. Dinner was fun but uneventful. I drove her home, kissed her goodnight, and that was it.

I think it was from that moment forward that I fell in love with Katrina. I still wasn't ready for a new relationship – this was definitely rebound territory. But I couldn't help myself.

I didn't have all that much time with Katrina. For a few short months, we'd go out almost every week. Dinner, hiking, sailing – all sorts of stuff. But there was a deadline looming. Early in our relationship, she had signed on to do a year-long sailboat race. It started at summer's end. Our summer. In that short time, I did what I could to move us from friends to lovers. Nothing worked. It was like she knew that I wasn't ready. In the end, there wasn't enough time.

Looking back. I think the elevator incident was a test. Katrina wanted to see if I was ready for something more than friendship. In her world, that test involved rough sex. When her elevator shenanigans weren't met with immediate reciprocation, she mentally moved on.

It's been over ten years now since Katrina and I were together. We've both had several relationships come and go but we've always kept in touch. As good friends do, we tell each other the truth. Both of us regret not taking our relationship to the next level when it was still new. Since then, the time has never seemed right for us to try again. One or the other of us has always been involved with someone else. We've both relocated several times and have never again lived in the same state. Life moves on. Fate doesn't always grant us a second chance.

I often think about those early days with Katrina and how things might have been different. If only I'd done things a bit differently. If I acted with the confidence that I have now but didn't have then. She might have been the love of my life. I'll never know. Unless….

I want a do-over.

## ABOUT THE AUTHOR

David lives in Florida with his wife, Claudia, and his two mini-Golden Doodles – Bentley and Maverick. Those cute little fur balls provide all the inspiration necessary for Chewy, our beloved and slightly cranky 11th Dimensional dog.